Cursing up the Wrong Tree

A HEX ON ME MYSTERY
BOOK TWO

KENNEDY LAYNE

IF THE CURSE FITS

DEDICATION

Jeffrey—You've always loved werewolf movies, so this story is just for you!

Cole—It's not a chupacabra, but it's close!

Witches, warlocks, and werewolves, oh my! Things get rather hairy in the next installment of the Hex on Me Mysteries by USA Today Bestselling Author Kennedy Layne...

Lou and the gang start out with every intention of tracking down a medium who they hope can speak to her ancestors and gain vital information in an effort to break the hex cast about by the only known immortal Lich Queen. They should have known their trip wouldn't quite go as planned.

Another vision that Lou has been cursed with comes to fruition, this time in the wilds of the Wyoming back country. What was the victim doing miles from civilization without adequate supplies? Residents in the neighboring town know more than they're saying, yet all the evidence points in a different direction.

Things are about to come to a head under the light of the full moon. You'll need to make sure you have a bit of silver in your pocket before joining Lou and the others for another mystifying whodunit...this one promises to have fangs!

Chapter One

THE GOLDEN SUN continued to climb over the horizon of the Midwestern state of Illinois as if it were any other morning. For most people, that would be completely ordinary. They would be hitting their snooze buttons on their alarm clocks two or three times, hoping for five more minutes of blissful sleep with each pause. Eventually, they'd accept their fate as typical drones and begin the routine of another mundane workday. Covers would be tossed to the side, the waking populace would grimace as the cool air of the bedroom hit their warm bodies, and then the soles of their feet would touch the chilly surface of the hardwood floor. They'd be left with that one nagging question—was today the day they'd throw in the towel and turn on their heaters?

Unfortunately…or not…I didn't have that problem.

I was no longer awakened by an alarm clock, I didn't own a nice house with beautiful hardwood floors, and I certainly no longer had my teaching job at a community college on the West Coast, which I had loved. No, having a normal existence would have been asking too much in this crazy, absurd life I was currently living.

You see, I was a cursed witch.

I'd never known there could be such a thing, and I certainly would never, ever have suspected I could be so unfortunate as to be one. Let me just say that it was now perfectly clear that the old adage *never say never* held a bit of sage advice.

Anyway, I'd needed a bit of fresh air, but it wasn't like I could go very far.

I was currently standing next to a cornfield watching the sun come up over the horizon. There were no cornstalks to block my view, considering that the fall harvest season had just ended. The now barren land looked much like what my life had become—free of any new growth. I wasn't the type to feel sorry for myself, but every now and then I needed a moment of privacy to decompress.

I'd found that reflection wasn't always a bad thing. It put things into perspective.

I shoved my hands into the pockets of my black leather jacket and lifted my face to the cold morning air in hopes that it would both reinvigorate me and help rid me of this massive headache.

Good luck with that, Miss Lilura. I need a spot of warm cream after that lovely vision.

"Pearl, what are you doing up at this time of the morning?" I asked the sleek white familiar who'd suddenly materialized beside me. She just had to bring up my most recent vision that was responsible for my current mood, didn't she? A quick glance at the brand-new RV that I'd invested three quarters of my trust fund into revealed that no one else was up and about on this early Friday morning. "And could we please dispense with the use of my surname? We've been traveling together for over a week. Can't you just call me Lou like everyone else?"

I'm not everyone. Just so you know, if I were to call you by any other title besides your given name, it would certainly not be a nickname that rhymes with goo…or the loo. You were born Tempest Darcinean Lilura. Have some small morsel of pride, dear hexed one.

What I needed was some peace and quiet away from my companions.

Want and need are two completely different things, my dear. A bit of humor can make life far more enjoyable, as I'm sure you know.

"You should go back to sleep for another hour or two," I suggested, thinking about the next twenty-four hours. Humor would have to wait until I was free of this hex the Lich Queen had bestowed upon me. "We have a long drive ahead of us, and we're all going to need our wits about us when we get there."

The *we* I was currently referring to was the warlock and another witch who'd chosen to help me with this impossible quest I'd set out to complete. Orwin Cornelia and Piper Allifair were literally helping me keep my sanity as this curse continued to take its toll. These past eight days had been the longest I'd gone without a vision of death.

A toll, Miss Lilura? Well, you've certainly managed to vastly understate the magnitude of our dilemma. I must say, it almost feels as if I've been rolled over by a steamroller. But I digress. Getting back to seeing the lighter side of things, it would behoove you to force a laugh once in a full moon.

The English-accented white familiar hailed back to the days of Cleopatra. The wise feline was about as prim and proper as you might think an English lady of title might expect. There wasn't a single white majestic hair out of place, and she had the most beautiful green eyes I'd ever seen on a cat. With that said, she was also a tad bit obsessed with etiquette...and now, apparently my lack of humor.

An important detail to know about Pearl was that she wasn't my familiar. She belonged to Piper, so the sage feline was technically compelled to follow Piper on this quest without a choice.

Don't believe for one moment, dear hexed one, that I did not have a choice. My sweet Piper might have a heart of gold, but even she can see reason when it is pointed out...especially by a familiar like me. Your predicament might have tugged on both of our heartstrings, which is why we are now in the middle of a cornfield just outside of Timbuktu. If it wasn't for the comforts afforded to us by our new transportation, I might be rethinking our decision. As for etiquette, we are civilized beings, are we not? We should act accordingly.

I'm not sure what incredibly naïve moment of weakness made me believe a few moments of alone time would make my so-called predicament seem less desperate. It was more than a predicament. I wasn't even sure one could call such a curse a predicament.

I was trying to be mindful of your feelings, my dear. I may have missed my mark. It does happen from time to time. However, if you'd been taught proper manners, you would have accepted my gesture.

The throbbing in my temples pounded even harder. Truth be told, I had trouble accepting more than a few slights these days, and I'll tell you why.

You see, I'd inadvertently encountered whom I believed to be an elderly witch over four months ago—only she hadn't been but a mere witch in centuries. No, Ammeline Letty Romilda was the legendary myth of the paranormal community that had been used for many, many years to keep little supernatural children in line within the covens. I'd found out the hard way that she wasn't just a character in an old wives' tale. If only they knew the truth, those children had every right to be scared.

A monster walked among us with the outward physical form of a sweet elderly woman.

Ammeline Letty Romilda *was* essentially immortal, and she was currently the only Queen Lich in existence to anyone's knowledge. I'd rather there be none, but that was a work in progress.

Of course, that would require that Ammeline's phylactery—a plain wooden cane she always carried with her—to be crushed against the well of time or any other standard method of destroying a magical artifact. Not your everyday milk run. Not by anyone's measure.

It's alright, my dear. Not everyone has perfect timing. After all, we're just mere supernatural beings.

"I was hexed with the foreshadowing of death, all because I said good morning to a thief who'd stolen Ammeline's cane—the same one that stores the source of all her power. I should have skipped my morning coffee that day."

Yes, that is true. If it makes you feel better to think bad timing was the sole factor responsible for your dilemma, it could have easily been someone else in your unfortunate situation. And one without the means to travel around the country in an attempt to save innocent people from passing through death's door prematurely. Fate does make sense if one stands far enough away to see the alternatives.

"You're just a lovely ray of sunshine, aren't you?" I asked wryly, giving up any hope for a moment alone. Nothing like a heavy dose of reality first thing in the morning just before getting on the road of one's destiny. It was just as well. We had a long day ahead of us and that wasn't going to change anytime soon. "Go ahead and wake up the others. They should know that we need to take a slight detour to Wyoming. We have a mystery to solve. As usual, time is of the essence."

Chapter Two

THE LONG BLACK strands of my hair whipped into my face when a gust of cold wind came across the harvested land. My eyes watered at the abrupt invasion, and it was a harsh reminder that winter wasn't far away. How many more mysteries would we be forced to solve by the end of the year? I wasn't sure how many more graphic visions I could take without losing my mind.

Which is why one shouldn't be alone after witnessing what was basically a horrible death. You seem to forget, my dear, that I am linked to all thoughts of witches and warlocks within range. That poor, poor man. What a horrible way to die. Although, I do believe my stomach has settled enough to enjoy a spot of warm cream now. I'm sure I can even summon the strength to tell you a knock-knock joke, if you'd like. Or maybe the one where a witch walks into a bar.

The only thing my stomach could handle right now was coffee. Apparently, I wasn't refined enough to bounce back as quickly as Pearl after having such explicit visions.

You grow accustomed to such things over the centuries.

Knock-knock.

"I'm not answering that door right now, Pearl."

I began the short trek back to the massive RV that pretty much held every convenience we could possibly need, given the circumstances. I had purchased a fifty-two foot long Powerhouse Custom Motor Coach in a multi-tone grey motif. It had four slide-outs, a Motorsports Sky Deck on the roof with internal access from the main cabin, and all the amenities we could want from a traveling home.

I must say, I am enjoying my soft bed near the skylight up front. It's very relaxing to view the twinkling stars at night and be awakened by the first rays of sunshine peeking over the horizon. I do not, however, appreciate being jarred from my sleep by a vision of a man being mauled to death.

I grimaced when I recalled the vivid imagery, as well. Maybe I'd forgo that cup of coffee for the moment. At the rate I was going, I'd end up with ulcers. I didn't have time for any unscheduled medical emergencies. If we weren't attempting to save someone from death, we were busy looking anywhere and everywhere for a remedy to this horrible hex I'd been cursed with by Ammeline.

"The guy we saw in the vision could still be alive, Pearl. We might still have time to reach him."

I pulled open the door to find that Orwin was already at his desk. His jet-black hair was sticking up every which way due to bedhead, and his black-rimmed glasses were a bit askew. He must not have put on the coffee, because the only aroma I could smell was the pumpkin spiced plug-in that Piper had bought on our last stop. She had a thing for pumpkins—pumpkin spiced coffee, pumpkin pie, pumpkin fragrances, you name it. I was about pumpkined out.

"Good morning, Orwin," I replied, regardless that we'd definitely had better mornings.

Orwin—my resident tech genius—must have just turned on his computer, because the red and white lights of his machine were still whirring to life. With the amount of research that needed to be done for my so-called predicament, there wasn't enough high-end computers nor bandwidth in the world at our disposal.

You're forgetting paranoid conspiracy theorist in your description, Miss Lilura. Have you thought about getting Mr. Cornelia some professional help?

"Time to reach who?" Orwin asked with a yawn, giving a cautious sideways glance to Pearl as she gracefully walked behind his chair toward the back of the RV as if she hadn't just tossed out an insult. He promptly sneezed three times in succession before being able to reach for a tissue, but he certainly hadn't missed Pearl's intention. "And I don't need professional help, Pearl. I could use some allergy shots, though. You just need to fess up that aliens did, in fact, land near the pyramids during your time as a kitten. I know you can hear me!"

I sighed in resignation at the ongoing feud between warlock and familiar. Orwin was highly allergic to anything with fur, but he adamantly refused to lower the protection ward he'd placed on himself to prevent him from ending up in my position.

I can't say I blamed him one bit.

It had taken Orwin close to two months to collect all the appropriate—and very rare—ingredients for such a powerful incantation. Witchcraft came in many different forms, but the heart of such abilities lay solely in the energy derived from earth.

"We need to make a detour." There was no use beating around the bush. I shrugged off my black leather jacket before hanging it up on the coat rack that I'd mounted onto the paneling of the RV near the door. The small antique piece we'd picked up in Kecksburg, Pennsylvania went perfect with the light oak décor, much to Piper's delight. Honestly, I had been surprised there wasn't a pumpkin carved into the wood. "Wyoming, to be more specific."

Orwin had tossed his used tissue into the wastebasket underneath his desk before reaching for his bottle of over-the-counter allergy medicine. With the large size of the RV, his allergies actually hadn't been too bad. Well, if you discounted when Pearl wanted to make a point of some sort or another. She sure had a spiteful nature when provoked, although I'm relatively sure it was all in good spirits.

"Good spirits?" Orwin asked as he pushed up his black-rimmed glasses. I might have forgotten to mention that he had the ability to read thoughts when he was within six feet of someone. Between him and Pearl, it was rare that Piper and I ever had a thought to ourselves. "That white sarcastic allergy-inducing feline is going to be the death of me. I'd rather go out by alien infestation, if given a choice."

"No such luck today, friend." I took a seat at the kitchen table that was surrounded by a very comfortable booth. I reached for my laptop, hoping to find the specific area we needed to go to in Wyoming. The smallest details in the visions that plagued me were like finding needles in a haystack. "Dying isn't on today's schedule, but a road trip is as soon as I can figure out what town we're headed to in Wyoming. I don't have a lot to go on."

Orwin allowed the silence to grow, knowing me well enough that I usually needed a bit of space after a vision. Pearl had yet to figure that out, but it was oddly comforting to know that I wasn't alone in my misery.

Don't get me wrong.

I wouldn't have bestowed this hex on my worst enemy, but there was something to be said for being among allies when things hit the fan.

"Do we have time left to save the victim?" Orwin asked quietly, having given me the time to start up my laptop and begin researching the small towns of Wyoming. He didn't need to expand on his question. I knew exactly what he meant, and I didn't have a definitive answer. We were at least seventeen hours out, if not more, from an area where the death I'd foreseen would happen within the next twenty-four hours. It was always a race against the clock, and we usually fell short of preventing the actual event from happening. "Tell me what you're looking for, and I'll see if I can put the parameters in the search engine I've been working on over the last two weeks."

I hated that I had to recall the most minuscule details of my visions, but every aspect of what I saw could literally mean the difference between life and death.

"A young man, probably in his mid-twenties, was driving on a back road at night. He was by himself and listening to a country radio station. His thumb was tapping on the steering wheel…almost as if he had some built-up nervous energy that he couldn't get rid of rather than in rhythm with the music. The clock on the dashboard read one-fifty-eight." I slowly took my fingers off the keyboard of my laptop and closed my eyes in an attempt to evoke the smallest of details. "There was hiking equipment in the back seat, along with a flashlight and a large caliber rifle. He had an energy drink in the cup holder, and something else lying on the front seat that I couldn't quite remember. I think he might have been going hunting. He pulled up to a spot that was surrounded by trees. Had he reached for the rifle in the back before opening his car door, he might have stood a chance of surviving. He was attacked, maybe by a large dog or a wolf, but there was a human silhouette standing in a small opening. I'm not sure if this was some sort of animal attack or his death was orchestrated, but I'll spare you the gory details."

"Wyoming is an awfully big state," Orwin pointed out, having spun in his chair to face his computer with a whistle. I'd ordered all the very expensive pieces on his shopping list, something about 4k and another thing to do with enough CPU processor cores to not bottleneck the graphics processing unit. Oh, and there was also something about RAM/Storage to manage something called a relational database written in something called SQL. It all sounded like gibberish to me, but it made him happy and produced top results on matters such as the one we were facing. "Anything else you can tell me?"

If I'm not mistaken, a small obscure campsite at least thirty miles north of Jackson.

"She's back," Orwin whispered with an arch of his black eyebrow. "Maybe if we ignore her, she'll go back to whatever cave she emerged from."

I'm sure it's possible with the technology that was left behind by the…oh, my. I'm not supposed to talk about my time navigating the pyramids. Forget I said anything, alien hunter.

Orwin's audible sigh of frustration carried throughout the camper, but that didn't stop him from tapping away on his mechanical keyboard. The loud tactile ticking sound had been quite irritating to begin with, but I'd gotten rather used to the noise.

Much like Pavlov's dog. Is your mouth watering yet?

I caught sight of Orwin's smile. He didn't have to say a word. I could tell that he was enjoying this moment far too much. For once, Pearl's witty remark wasn't directed toward him. Piper must not have given Pearl her *spot of warm cream* yet. It was really hard not to mentally say that phrase and not have it come out with an English accent.

I was not attempting to bedazzle you with my witty banter, Miss Lilura. I was just pointing out that the sound of Mr. Cornelia's mechanical keyboard usually produces results that cause you to react. You associate the sound with vital information. That is not a bad thing, unless you count the times Mr. Cornelia has used his impeccable skills to waste our time trying to prove that aliens do indeed exist.

"Impeccable?" Orwin repeated in somewhat disbelief, swiveling his chair around with an even broader smile. "Did you just give me a compliment, Pearl? I wasn't paying attention."

Pearl gracefully jumped up on the counter next to the refrigerator without making a sound. Orwin's lopsided grin began to slowly fade as the last of Pearl's declaration penetrated his caffeine-deprived brain.

"Wait. Are you admitting that aliens have visited earth? Lou, are you hearing this?"

I do see your value, Mr. Cornelia. With that said, I never confirmed nor denied that your little green friends exist. I only meant that you were doing your best to prove such a thing happened. Now, my sweet Piper has always been slow to face the day. Would you be so kind as to pour some cream into my saucer and warm it in the microwave for exactly twenty-one seconds, Miss Lilura?

"How do you know the place we're looking for is north of Jackson?" I asked with complete curiosity. Granted, Pearl could see my visions when I experienced one, and she wasn't affected nearly as much as I was during the prophecy. Was she able to pick up details that I couldn't? That would definitely give us an advantage going forward. "There were no signs on the road that the victim took, nor were there any mile markers."

"Morning," Piper interrupted with a mumble, her blonde hair stacked high on top of her head in a messy bun. It didn't surprise me anymore to see her come out from the back bedroom in flannel pajamas. Honestly, I didn't even know that people still wore them until our first night in the RV. She even had the matching fuzzy slippers to complete the ensemble. "What has Pearl so worked up? She was going on and on about her cream and the upcoming trip. Didn't we decide we were leaving at nine?"

As I mentioned, my sweet Piper takes her sweet time waking up.

I'd already poured Pearl's cream into her saucer, but I didn't have to respond after Piper rubbed the sleep out of her eyes. Her blue gaze landed on each and every one of us, guessing correctly that another vision had taken place.

She is an exceptionally smart one, but my sweet Piper

does function better on coffee. Would you please hit the brew
button on the coffee maker, Miss Lilura?

"What about the witch in Minnesota?" Piper asked,
rightly concerned that we would be postponing what
could possibly be a golden ticket to the cure for my hex.
"I've been helping Orwin research her lineage, and
there's a good chance she has the ability to speak with
our ancestors in the afterlife. She could be the ultimate
secret weapon we've been looking for."

"She'll have to wait until we knock this next case
out," Orwin replied with a small shrug, having done this
same routine with me more times than I could count.
We'd gotten used to changing our plans in the blink of
an eye. "We still have time to save this man's life, but the
number of campsites north of Jackson is beyond
astounding. We're going to need something more to
narrow our search, like maybe a site number."

Look for campsites that have had an increase in recent
animal attacks, ol' alien hunter. It shouldn't be too hard.
That will be our destination.

Piper plopped into the booth at the kitchen table.
The fact that we wouldn't be talking to the medium
until another murder mystery was wrapped up was hard
for her to accept. The struggle was real. I set Pearl's
saucer in the microwave, completely aware that she was
monitoring the buttons I pressed to make sure it was
exactly twenty-one seconds.

I disagree, dear hexed one. Yes, you were cursed with the
prophecy of murders, but you should not look upon this as a

bother. You have the ability to save a life. Don't you think that the victims' loved ones are thankful for those you've saved over the last four months? You were able to save the café manager in my sweet Piper's hometown. I'm sure if her parents had been aware that they might have not been able to spend another second with their daughter, they would worship at your feet. May I remind you that I've seen this type of thing before. Cleopatra was deserving of such worship, mind you.

"Oh, yeah," Orwin replied with a snap of his fingers, most likely to help me out from a very complex answer. I understood what Pearl was saying, but it was still a hard pill to swallow. "I keep forgetting that you're an old lady. Exactly how old are you?"

Did you miss your elementary lesson in manners, alien hunter? Never, ever ask a female her age. The consequences of failing to heed that particular rule are not pretty.

"What if the medium can really talk to our lost family members?" Piper asked, drawing everyone's attention her way before this particular quarrel got out of hand. We could always count on her being the peacemaker. "Can we really afford to pass up that opportunity? Listen, your Jeep is hooked to the back of the RV. Pearl and I can take a drive up to Minnesota and see if this witch is the real deal, while you and Orwin drive to Wyoming."

My red Jeep was my prized possession, and my heart beat hard against my chest at the thought of being separated from her. I mean, I was also concerned with

Piper and Pearl gallivanting around on their own, but my Jeep?

We are not, I repeat not separating from the group only to find ourselves in different states. I find myself in dire need of that warm cream, Miss Lilura.

I could totally relate with Pearl regarding this stressful situation, and she had a right to be worried. Once I'd slid the warm saucer over to her on the counter, I promptly pressed the brew button on the coffee machine that Orwin had already pre-filled before bed last night. I was going to need all the fuel I could get to make it through the next twenty-four hours.

Piper was new to this way of life. Orwin and I had basically become hunters since my curse. Piper and Pearl? Not so much. I certainly didn't want to be responsible should anything happen to them. As Pearl had already mentioned…families tended to take things personal when it came to a loved one. I'd already upset one immortal being in my relatively short lifetime. I truly didn't need an entire family of witches hunting me down, as well.

"Um, Lou?"

I closed my eyes when Orwin said my name in that cautious manner that could only mean one thing—he'd found something.

It was no doubt regarding the site he'd been searching for, and it wasn't simply the location. He'd discovered something else that I wasn't going to like in the least.

Mr. Cornelia certainly has a way of causing apprehension, doesn't he?

"I can hear the two of you," Orwin complained again, having turned around in his chair to face us. He used his thumb to indicate his computer behind him. "I found the campsite. There was indeed a couple of unusual animal attacks in the area."

The coffee was taking too long, so I quickly exchanged the carafe for a mug. Maybe it was time I started drinking the rich beverage in its natural form straight into one of my veins. Who needed sugar or half-and-half when one could get his or her coffee intravenously?

We all need our measure of creamer, my dear. It soothes the soul. And from the look on Mr. Cornelia's face, you'll be in need of that soon. Remember, I can always resort to telling the witch walked into a bar joke.

"What am I missing?" Piper asked, having not been awake long enough to have heard the entire conversation about the man I'd seen die a horrible death. "An animal attack? I thought you said someone was murdered."

"Someone *was* murdered," Orwin said before joining me at the counter. He took the mug out from under the stream of dark liquid and put the carafe back in its place before sliding the half-filled ceramic cup in front of me. "Drink up, Lou. I don't think that the man you saw in your vision was attacked by the local wildlife, if you get my drift. We might very well be dealing with a pack of werewolves."

Chapter Three

"I HAVE TO tell you," Piper murmured, falling into step with me as we entered a gas station on the edge of a small town around twenty miles out from the campsite. "These people aren't too friendly. That woman drove off so darn fast, she almost ran over my foot barreling past me."

"I noticed the look we got." It was closing in on one o'clock in the morning, leaving us roughly an hour to save a man's life. It had been a tough break for the novice members of our team to be thrown into such a dangerous case. It seemed our luck had turned for the worse, and we were stuck dealing with huge musclebound creatures, complete with needle-sharp fangs and razor-sharp claws. "Maybe she was just tired and wanted to get home after a long second shift. Either way, can you feel the undercurrent of supernatural energy here? I detected it the moment we drove into this tiny town."

"Yes." Piper used the cantrip we'd practiced in the practical defense training I'd been going over with her this past week, and I could literally see her take in every detail of our surroundings. There was an elderly male cashier at the register, a male patron who appeared to be coming off of second shift as a security guard, and another employee stocking soda cans in the back. "It's almost an edgy kind of energy…almost electrical."

The same type of energy I'd gotten off the victim in my vision. I don't believe it was electrical so much as it stemmed from fear. That particular emotion had a prickly texture to it when sensed by a receptive medium or witch.

"It's like the residents are scared of something," I whispered back, snagging a chocolate candy bar from one of the end caps. This was technically Piper's first case since we'd left her hometown. I was quite pleased with how she was handling herself. "Would you please grab me a bottle of water? I'm going to look at the chargers. Mine's been on the fritz lately."

I'd raised my voice so that anyone listening would think we were just regular customers. It wasn't like we had an automatic antenna for other supernatural beings or them for us. We usually found out the hard way if there was another witch, vampire, or werewolf within our vicinity. Given the amount of animal attacks in the area, I was with Orwin on this one—there might be a pack of werewolves setting up residence in this out-of-the-way village north of Jackson, Wyoming. The creatures might be preying on the tourists camping in the area.

We'd spent the last eighteen hours taking turns driving while researching the area, the terrain, and what other facts we could gather from the news sites regarding the strange recent string of animal attacks. Orwin had used his computer skills to discover that three other similar incidents had occurred within a two-month span.

Mason Leeds, Clyde Simmons, and Russell Sutter had their lives taken within the last eight weeks. Piper had pulled up their photographs, but none had been the man I'd seen in my vision. Was there a specific reason these men had been targeted? Or had they just been in the wrong place at the wrong time?

Piper had spent most of her time trying to search social media sites for any family connections to the victims, hoping I'd recognize the man I'd seen in my vision. She had the right idea that it could be a brother or cousin looking for revenge against an animal that probably didn't even exist…at least, if our assumption was right that this had more to do with werewolves than it did with the natural wildlife in the surrounding area. This kind of back country had a plentiful supply of its own predators, but most wildlife tended to shy away from humans out of instinct.

"Can I help you find something?"

The older man behind the cash register had been monitoring my movements, which wasn't very surprising. Given the time of night, it was highly doubtful that he got a lot of customers.

"I'm just looking over your selections of phone

chargers," I said with a smile, grabbing the first one I saw off the rack and holding it up in victory.

"Pretty late to go looking for a phone charger, wouldn't you say?" the man asked before putting a toothpick in between his lips. He watched me a little too closely. "You're not from around these parts, are you?"

"We're on our way to join a friend up north of here to do some camping." I'd kept as close to the truth as I could, not knowing exactly who I was dealing with—human or supernatural being. As I'd experienced most recently, even what seemed like the sweetest old lady could turn into the vilest creature on the face of the planet. "We're taking turns driving. I've got to tell you, that RV was the best investment I ever made."

The older man didn't bother to look out the display window where Orwin was busy filling up the gas tank on the beast of a vehicle. Technically, there were two seventy-five gallon tanks. Instead, the man's cloudy blue eyes remained trained directly on me.

I tried to maintain a friendly demeanor as I spoke again.

"My name is Lou." I slowly walked over to the cash register, setting down the chocolate bar and the phone charger that I'd only end up giving to Orwin. Piper had yet to join me with that bottle of water, which meant she'd been successful in engaging the teenage stock boy into a conversation. I could only hope she was having better luck than me. "We've been taking the scenic route, and I've got to say this neck of the woods doesn't disappoint. It's beautiful countryside."

"Hey, Jasper. How's it going?"

The security guard, still in uniform, had one of those prewrapped sandwiches in his hand with a bottle of Coke. I figured he was in his mid-twenties, but he wasn't the man I'd seen in my vision. At least this resident seemed friendlier than the rest, unlike his neighbors.

"Matt," the older man repeated with a nod after shifting his toothpick to the side of his mouth.

"Oh, let me move these out of the way," I offered politely to Matt, sliding my two items to the side on the counter so that the security guard's purchases could be rung up. "I'm waiting for my friend to finish shopping."

"Thank you, ma'am," Matt replied, looking over his shoulder with a grin. "Your friend might be a while. Good ol' Chucky is probably talking her ear off. Jasper here isn't much for conversation, so you can imagine how quiet it is in here this time of night."

Jasper grunted, although I wasn't sure he was agreeing with the security guard or if that was his way of joining the discussion.

"I was just telling Jasper that you have beautiful countryside out this way."

"I take it that's your RV outside," Matt guessed correctly, though it wasn't like there was any other strange vehicle in the parking lot. He'd taken out his wallet and tossed a five-dollar bill on the counter. "A bit of advice—

don't go to any of the campgrounds close around here. I know it's pretty late, but you and your friends might want to drive a good sixty or eighty miles north from here before you decide to stop for the night."

"Oh?" I asked, giving my best perplexed expression. Jasper had taken the five and pushed some buttons on what could only be described as an antique cash register. The drawer opened with a ding. "Why is that? I'd think this area would have the best campsites within driving distance of the town."

"There's been a few animal attacks recently. The park rangers are doing their best to warn the campers not to leave food out and to take precautions. I wouldn't venture too far out into those woods without a loaded rifle or two. Honestly, a shotgun might not get the trick done." Matt took back the dollar and a few pennies that Jasper had laid on the counter next to the prewrapped sandwich and can of Coke. He then tossed the change into the "take one" tray. "They're thinking maybe it's a lone wolf that's gotten territorial or even a couple of females protecting their litters. It's not like they're starving for food out in these neck of the woods, but you never know. Maybe a large male got hurt and can't hunt its usual prey. Humans are slow and relatively less dangerous than a mule deer."

"I don't know why everyone is all worked up," Jasper exclaimed in a raspy voice that gave away the fact he smoked...and quite a lot from the sound of it. He hadn't even moved from his spot on the stool to ring up Matt's order. "Animal attacks like these happen once every five years or so. That lone wolf will move on sooner or later. Mark my words."

"Brady Buchanan's nephew was one of the victims, Jasper," Matt pointed out with a frown, clearly disappointed in Jasper's opinion on the subject. "Tommy didn't deserve to die like that. I heard his family is rallying a big hunt for tomorrow, but the park rangers will probably stop them before they get too far into the woods. Hunting greys is illegal nowadays. The federal boys get a bit touchy about us locals going anywhere near the endangered species around here, and with good reason considering it's their job to protect the wolves."

Matt picked up his purchases that Jasper hadn't bothered to put in a bag. The security guard gave me an apologetic smile and a small shrug.

"I'm sorry, ma'am. We're a small close-knit community, and we've lost one of our own." Matt tapped the counter as he went to take his leave. "You take care now. Don't venture too far from the fire."

"I'm so sorry," I said sincerely, watching as Matt walked out the door. Had I been mistaken? Was Tommy the young man I'd seen in my vision? I didn't recall the name being in the list of victims, so it was a good possibility that we were too late. "I didn't mean to upset him."

"Tommy's funeral is tomorrow afternoon," Jasper

fessed up, reaching forward and sliding my two items closer to him. His hazy blue eyes focused on Piper over my shoulder, but she was still talking with the stock boy. "The family is grieving and needs something to blame. The park rangers need to do their job before someone else gets hurt. Chucky, stop gossiping back there and do your job!"

Tommy's funeral was tomorrow? Then he couldn't have been the young man I'd seen in my vision. At least, I didn't think that could happen. A day or two at the most, maybe. But I've never experienced a foreshadowing that had anything to do with the past that far back. Wouldn't that be a misnomer? Anyway, I still couldn't recall seeing that name anywhere in the list of victims.

"You really think it was just a lone wolf attacking those campers?" I asked, my frown genuine. Jasper mentioned that this kind of thing happened every five or so years. I'd mentioned that detail to Orwin. Maybe he could find a connection within the timeline. "Please tell Matt I said thanks for the advice on the campsites. I'll let my friends know what's going on in the area."

Werewolves were still part human, and they typically only changed during the full moon. That didn't mean one couldn't manage the strength to change at will, but for the most part they lived among townsfolk in various remote towns like this, and no one was ever the wiser. Why would they risk outing themselves to the general population of such a small village? And every five years?

It just didn't make any sense.

There was a generic clock on the wall behind Jasper. Around eight minutes had passed since Piper and I had walked into the gas station. We shouldn't waste any more time before we headed out. It was best we get a move on and make it to the campsite where we believed the murder would take place. We had the means to protect ourselves, provided we used caution.

"You have a great employee in Chucky, sir," Piper said with a smile as she came to stand beside me, plopping two bottles of water on the counter. "He was just telling me about the local diner and how they have the best omelets for breakfast. Lou, I think we should stay at one of the local campgrounds and try out that diner. It's pretty late, and we're all tired. A good breakfast will get our road trip off to a good start in the morning."

Jasper didn't say a word of caution as he rang up our items, nodding toward the cash register's black and white numbers that read a little over twelve dollars. I had a feeling that the charger I bought wouldn't last me a week.

"Jasper and the man who just left here were telling me about a couple of animal attacks in the area," I shared with her, thinking she probably got the same information from Chucky. It was hard not to think of the cult classic horror film with a name like that. "I'm not so sure we should stay around here. It might not be safe."

"Well, let's run it past Orwin. It's not like we'd be sleeping in tents," Piper pointed out with a shrug, exactly as I would have done had I been given the chance. It would certainly explain our presence in town come tomorrow morning. I'd handed over a twenty-dollar bill, not even sure this gas station took credit cards with the exception of their gas pumps. "Lou, why don't I meet you outside? I'm going to talk with Orwin."

Piper's words seemed a little rushed together, but she was gone before I could say another word. A quick glance revealed that she'd made a beeline for the glass door.

"Your friend is right, you know." Jasper went the extra mile and began to store the items we'd purchased into a flimsy plastic bag. I wasn't so sure it wouldn't give way before I made my way outside, but it was still a kind gesture. "You have that big RV. It's not like a lone grey wolf can work a doorknob. They might be clever, but they aren't that sharp."

I had a feeling that Jasper wasn't a huge fan of the Buchanan family, but I don't believe he was trying to throw me or my friends under the bus...or in this case, RV. He truly didn't seem too worried about the attacks. Then again, he was probably in his late seventies. I'm sure he'd seen a lot during his good old days roaming around these parts.

"It's true that the RV is a secure place to sleep," I replied, shoving the change of my twenty dollars in the right pocket of my black leather jacket. I wasn't one to carry a purse the way Piper did, because it just slowed me down. Everything I needed was in my phone case, which I carried in my jacket. "We might just hunker down for the night and enjoy a hearty breakfast at the diner come morning. You have a good night, Jasper."

I'm pretty sure Jasper rewarded me with a grunt, but I couldn't hear him over the ringing in my ears. You see, I'd turned on my knee-high boots to head for the exit when I caught sight of a familiar Land Rover at one of the pumps. The artificial lights above hit the driver's side window just right to cause a glare, preventing me from seeing the driver inside. I tried to tell myself it was just a coincidence, and that this particular vehicle could belong to just about anyone.

There was only one problem with that scenario—I wasn't big on coincidences anymore.

On our last case, a very mysterious man had somehow inserted himself into our investigation. He'd quickly disappeared after it was over, and I honestly thought it would be the last we'd ever see or hear from him again.

Apparently, I'd been wrong.

I never took my focus off the Land Rover as my hand pushed open the door. By the time I'd stepped outside into the cool air, the driver had stepped out. Even now, his roguishly handsome appeal was hard to miss, especially with those chiseled features and his five o'clock shadow. He also still wore that brown leather bomber jacket as if it were a protective skin.

Knox Emeric made no qualms about meeting my stare head on, only this time I knew his secret—he was a werewolf.

Chapter Four

"DON'T," PIPER WARNED softly, having cut off my advance toward Knox. She gently laid a hand on my arm and wouldn't let go until I looked directly at her. The coolness of the night practically burned my eyes, much like it had this morning. "Knox will undoubtedly follow us after he's done filling up his vehicle. We can talk to him then, but seeing as we don't know why he's here...I don't think we should let on to the locals that we know him."

Piper's blue gaze flicked over my shoulder to where Jasper was no doubt watching all of us very closely. It was probably relatively rare that he got two out-of-towners pumping gas at this time of night, and I'm sure he kept an eye on everyone passing through this area.

"How are you so certain that Knox will follow us?" I asked cautiously, while at the same time being pleasantly surprised that Piper was coming into her own and asserting her opinion. Had she already spoken to Knox? "He's disappeared on us once. His presence alone confirms that we're dealing with more than one werewolf. For all we know, he could be the one responsible for these murders."

"I might not have known you as long as Orwin has, but I know you well enough that you'd have Knox hogtied in a split second if you thought that the man was a murderer." Piper dropped her hand and tilted her head toward the RV with a small smile. "Orwin gestured toward Knox when he pulled into the gas station. They did that man thing, where they silently communicate through head nods. Trust me, Knox will follow us out to the campsite."

I reluctantly adjusted my path and started to make my way toward the RV while Knox began to fill up the fuel tank on his Land Rover as if nothing was amiss. It was almost like déjà vu all over again. When Orwin and I had made our way toward Bedford, Pennsylvania in hopes that Piper would be able to use her healing powers to cure me of this hex, we'd seen Knox at a gas station just outside of town. He'd then shown up at the café where Piper worked, claiming he'd been in search of a place with free Wi-Fi. I hadn't believed him then, and I'm not so sure I'd believe any excuse he'd come up with tonight.

Orwin and I never did find out the real reason Knox had been following us, and it looked as if we'd need to wait a little longer. We had more important things to worry about...like saving a man's life.

"We can't worry about Knox Emeric right now," I

advised, making an executive decision. I finally closed the distance to the RV. Orwin was nowhere in sight, telling me he was probably already behind the wheel waiting on us. "Let's load up. If Knox follows us as he's indicated he will…well, we'll deal with him when the time comes. A man's life hangs in the balance, and we didn't come all this way to fall a yard short of the goal line."

Piper fell into step beside me, and it wasn't long before she closed the door behind us. I quickly made my way to the front cabin, immediately looking through the windshield to take in our surroundings. Knox was still standing in between his vehicle and the gas pump, Jasper was on his stool behind the cash register inside the station, and the stock boy had made his way to the front. Chucky was staring outside in interest, probably wondering why us out-of-towners would be transiting the area so late at night.

"I know what you're thinking, but Emeric doesn't strike me as the type of man to kill someone without good reason," Orwin said quietly, his hands resting on the steering wheel.

Mr. Emeric isn't just a mere man, Mr. Cornelia. He's a werewolf.

"And he somehow knew that I was a warlock the last time we met, which tells me that he's been monitoring Lou and me for a while. And Pearl, you know you're not supposed to be up here," Orwin complained, shifting the RV into drive. He pulled the large vehicle out from the gas station ever so slowly, taking us right past Knox Emeric's Land Rover. He didn't even bother to glance up, and I'm sure he did so by design so that anyone watching him wouldn't know of his interest in us. "Go back from whence you came from, Egyptian pud-tat."

Drive, Mr. Cornelia. We have places to be and a life to save, if you don't mind.

"I agree with Orwin. I'm not sure how Knox can be involved in these murders." Piper was still standing behind Orwin as he maneuvered the RV onto the narrow road ahead. Pearl surprised me by gracefully hopping up into my lap after I'd taken a seat in the passenger side. "The animal attacks have been going on for weeks. Two weeks ago, Knox was in Bedford, Pennsylvania with us."

My sweet Piper does have a point.

"Werewolves usually travel in packs," I reminded all of them, stroking my hand down Pearl's back as I peered into the side mirror of the RV. We were driving slow enough that I could still watch as Knox set the gas nozzle back into place. "Knox Emeric could easily be from Wyoming, although his license plate does read Washington. Either way, we can't worry about him now unless he inserts himself into tonight's activities."

A quick glance at the clock over the radio read that it was now one-thirty-two. We'd figured out that two campsites have been the place of attacks, but one stood out from the satellite images that Orwin had been able to pull from somewhere. I'd come to the conclusion it was best not to ask any questions if I didn't want to listen to some long-winded explanation.

That was wise, dear hexed one.

As long as we weren't going to be hunted down by the government internet overlords, I could let things slide.

Well....

"Are we sticking to the plan?" Piper asked, planting her brown knee-high boots shoulder-width apart so that she could balance easier. She had on a matching peacock coat, with a multicolored scarf tucked underneath the lapels. She'd have to lose the accessory if she were to leave the RV. It was too easy to spot with the golden-brown threads. "I'll be up top on the platform. Pearl, remember that you're taking the high ground outside."

I wouldn't have it any other way, my sweet. I'm not made for roughing it in nature. If I'd wanted that, I would have chosen a different form of being.

"You get a choice?" Orwin asked in somewhat of a shocked tone before he leaned forward over the steering wheel after a single sneeze. He must have doubled up on his allergy medicine. Pearl wasn't the only thing he was allergic to out in these woods. "Lou, we're coming up on the turn."

Plan A hinged on whether or not there were any park rangers in the area. The last attack occurred at a campsite around two miles from here, so we were banking that was where they'd have a heavier presence. I would exit the RV right when we made the turn. I'd go deep into the woods and come around to where I'd seen the silhouette of a male figure. As Piper had already disclosed, Pearl would climb one of the trees on the edge of the forest to have a better vantage point, while Orwin would feign working on a tire. As for Piper, she would take the Skydeck, which was near fourteen feet off the ground.

Plan B would be for Orwin to utilize a bit of magic should a park ranger be guarding this particular campsite. It wouldn't do for a human to realize there was more than met the eye with regards to these animal attacks.

Headlights appeared behind us right as Orwin flipped on his turn signal.

Well, we certainly didn't include Mr. Emeric into the various plan iterations, now did we?

"No," I murmured, shifting so that I could set Pearl on the floor. "Orwin, don't hesitate to drive to the campsite once I'm out the door. Everyone armed?"

Armed is rather dramatic word for an ampoule of potion, wouldn't you agree?

Pearl was referring to the vial that was tied to a leather string, which Piper had slipped over her blonde hair so that it was safely tucked inside her peacock coat. The small vessel contained components that would activate once the compound liquid hit with air, putting whoever or whatever was after her to sleep for a good thirty minutes.

Orwin had a similar magical ampoule in his pocket, as did I. We had no intentions of hurting or killing anyone or anything. Quite the contrary, considering our business was saving lives. That did not mean we didn't recognize the dangerous stakes when dealing with supernatural creatures such as a rogue werewolf or a pack of them. Orwin did have a unique antique silver knife that he never went anywhere without attached to his belt for when a situation became a bit hairy in case I wasn't around to intervene.

Me? I had all the power I needed at my fingertips with my gift of telekinesis.

"Good luck, everyone," I murmured, slipping past Piper as she gave me a pat on the shoulder. It didn't take me long to exit the RV and slip into the shadows. Orwin didn't hesitate, stepping on the gas and gracefully advancing the large vehicle down a dirt and gravel road to the destination point. It was showtime. "Come on, Knox. Turn."

Sure enough, Knox's Land Rover slowed down, though he hadn't bothered to use his turn signal. I stepped out from the obscurity of the numerous trees the moment he turned onto the small dirt road, placing myself directly in the middle of his path.

Knox brought his vehicle to a complete stop within inches from me.

Our small standoff didn't last long.

He immediately cut his lights, descending me once

again into darkness. It was rather odd, but not once did I sense he was a danger to me. It had nothing to do with the fact that I could defend myself against a mere werewolf. No, the others were right. Knox Emeric didn't strike me as a killer, and he also didn't strike me as someone who would condone one of his own taking the lives of humans.

Be aware, he's not the only werewolf in the vicinity. And you'd be wise not to underestimate his strength, dear hexed one.

"Pearl, I told you not to do that," I muttered, hoping that Knox hadn't noticed the slight startled jump to my otherwise still stance. Doubtful, considering the branches of the trees diminished what moonlight was shining down from the sky above. "Why aren't you with the others?"

Mr. Cornelia is parking that elegant monstrosity, and I thought my presence might be desired here.

"How far away is the werewolf we're about to confront?" I asked, slowly walking toward the vehicle while keeping a wide berth.

Around eight hundred yards, give or take. And you should have used the plural version of that word. I smell a pair. It turns out that silhouette you saw in your vision might very well be a werewolf as we'd predicted. They are rather fast in their wolf form, aren't they?

This was the first real case that Orwin and I were able to work with Piper and Pearl. I've got to admit, it was nice having an ace up my sleeve in the form of a highly intelligent familiar. She had more knowledge about the supernatural in the tip of her tail than we all did combined together.

Oh, I do have my talents, dear hexed one. You take care of your Mr. Emeric while I keep a lookout for any more unwanted visitors.

I was maybe ten feet from the driver's side door of Knox's Land Rover when he finally rolled down his window. I'd already seen him at the gas station, but we hadn't been this close. It was hard to deny that the man had a charismatic presence. His golden eyes practically glowed in the darkness as his gaze landed on me.

"A coincidence, perhaps?" I asked, arching my brow. I'd gathered my hair at the base of my neck to prevent it from getting in the way should I end up in a hand-to-hand battle tonight. The only time that could happen was if someone was able to ambush me, but Pearl had my back. "I'm pretty sure you know my feelings on that word, Mr. Emeric."

"You made that abundantly clear at our last meeting," Knox replied, his deep voice chasing away any chill that had been in the air. I steeled myself against the unwanted reaction, wanting nothing to do with this man, wolf, or the reason he continued to show up at the most random places. "I guess I owe you an apology."

Such a smart man. I mean, werewolf.

"Not needed." I remained where I was, not foolish enough to get close to his vehicle should he try something underhanded. He'd figured out that I knew what he was, but he'd somehow discovered that I wasn't a mere human, either. "We're strangers. Your business is your own. Mine is my own. Let's keep it that way. The only thing I'm concerned about right now is the fact that you're interfering with our attempt at saving a man's life. Unless…"

Knox had rested an elbow on his window, keeping both hands on the wheel in a blatant attempt to put me at ease. That wasn't going to happen, and he seemed to sense it. He lifted his left hand and rubbed his thumb against his chin in contemplation.

He's trying to distract you, Miss Lilura.

"I've had nothing to do with the animal attacks that have been taking place for the last eight weeks. I'm here for the same reason you are," Knox confessed quietly, his gaze intently scanning our surroundings through the windshield. "I heard about the string of attacks and put two and two together. I came to see if I can stop whatever is happening in this town."

Oh, Mr. Emeric is good with the charm. I'll give him that.

"These attacks aren't just taking place on the full moon." I didn't want to be caught standing here when the male victim ventured inside the campsite. He might drive off, thereby not allowing us to question him. We needed information that only he had, especially if he knew what was hunting him. Granted, having him drive away would inadvertently save his life...for the time being. "One...no, actually two...of yours have gone rogue."

You've got him there, Miss Lilura. I'm rather enjoying this back and forth banter.

"Or someone is making it appear that way," Knox countered, dropping his hand. "I can help with whatever you're about to do."

How generous of our benefactor.

I quickly realized that Knox wasn't aware someone was due to die in probably five minutes, which gave me the advantage. It might be to our benefit to send him on some wild goose chase. Then again, we were in a precarious situation. Another set of eyes, ears, and claws might be beneficial.

A word of caution, dear hexed one—Mr. Emeric is one of them, not us.

"How far away are they?" I asked, hoping to receive two answers. There was only one way I could find out if Knox was somewhat trustworthy. "Your friends...how far are they from this area?"

I like the way you think, Miss Lilura. The answer would be four hundred yards or so closing fast on a parallel path toward the campsite.

"I'd prefer you don't refer to these scallywags as my friends. And the answer to your question is about four hundred yards upwind, give or take," Knox replied honestly after he'd carefully inhaled the cool air through his nose. "To clarify, I have no relationship with this pack. Friends or otherwise."

I had a decision to make, and it was one that needed to be made quickly.

Sooner would be better. Those furry creatures do have good hearing, too. Piper has already used an incantation to cover our scents. If you do decide for Mr. Emeric to join us temporarily, you should know that a rather important part of his senses will be hampered.

"Keep driving until you come to the RV," I instructed, taking my gaze off Knox long enough to scan what the locals considered the main road out of town. "Park behind it and make it seem as if you're offering Orwin assistance. I'll be coming in from the opposite direction."

Without another word, I stepped back into the shadows. Knox didn't even bother to roll up his window as he drifted forward, keeping the headlights turned off. One, the absence of glass no longer hindered his hearing. Two, those golden eyes of his could see better in the dark than what any incandescent light could offer to illuminate.

I hope you know what you're doing, Miss Lilura.

"You mean the fact that I might have just let the enemy into our camp?" I murmured, mindful that those werewolves were most likely close enough to pick up any type of verbal conversation. "I'm not one for taking chances, Pearl, but my outlook kind of changed after I was cursed by the Queen Lich."

Well, then. Shall we see if we can save that man's life? I do believe you are due for a win.

Chapter Five

*Y*OUR WEREWOLVES ARE *getting closer.*

Those creatures certainly weren't my were-wolves, but I understood what Pearl had meant to say. I remained silent, listening intently for any sign that I wasn't alone in my immediate vicinity. Pearl had taken the high ground, her English-accented voice coming from somewhere up above me. She had a clear view of the entire campsite.

Mr. Emeric is currently aiding Mr. Cornelia with one of the RV's tires, just as you requested.

I tilted my wrist just so in order to read the hands on my watch, waiting to catch a lone beam of moonlight.

One minute remained.

This is rather tantalizing, isn't it? Preparing for an impending raid? Reminds me of the old days.

Raid?

Pearl was definitely thinking way back to her World War II days and the raids over London. The way I looked at our current situation was that we'd already changed the outcome of the future. The man about to amble into an ambush at the campsite wouldn't be welcomed by a werewolf and a silhouette of a human.

No, the potential victim would have company in the form of two witches, a warlock, and ironically…another werewolf who seemed to genuinely want to prevent this incident. The man's death wouldn't unravel the way I'd seen in my vision, and that in and of itself was a win in my book of pluses and minuses.

It was way too often that Orwin and I didn't make it to save an innocent victim, so my relief was most welcome. Making it to the crime scene was always the hardest part of the case, and now that particular conflict was out of the way.

Headlights.

The artificial beams slowly drifted across one of the creatures, though I doubt the driver had caught sight of the werewolf. I'd known he was near, but it was still a jolt to lay eyes on the beast. Unlike how the romantic movies portray them, authentic werewolves were exactly that—a morphed beast that stood like a man but resembled a wolf with immense proportions. It remained hidden just along the edge of the tree line, but I was now within a hundred yards of the supernatural animal.

He's brave. His intention was to kill, but he's hesitating with the amount of people he's sensing. He's most likely questioning how he could have mistaken the scent of human beings. It won't be long before he realizes that the reason lies within the magical realm.

The creature could easily take two mortal men, but

something was holding it back. Knox's scent had been hidden, and Piper remained out of sight. It would have made it easier to capture the rogue beast had he advanced closer toward Orwin, giving me a better advantage.

Unfortunately, the potential victim had finally arrived in the exact same spot as in my vision. Would this beast attempt to attack all three men?

The second werewolf is beating a hasty retreat, Miss Lilura.

Pearl wasn't the only one who'd caught the departure. Before I could even lift my boot off the ground, the creature I had within my sights quickly lifted his snout and sniffed the air. My chance of stopping anymore attacks was dwindling rather rapidly, and I had to act fast.

I quickly advanced forward, knowing full well the beast would be able to hear my footsteps. There was no avoiding my obvious intent, but I was able to cut off his exit. I'd gone head to head with a werewolf just like this one over a month ago, but the previous one had clearly been rogue and his intentions had been evident.

There was something different about the creature standing in front of me.

Be careful, dear hexed one. Even I can sense this one's innate power.

The one standing before me snarled, but it didn't react without thinking. Instead, he stood there staring at me in all his glory. Was he wondering why I wasn't intimidated in his presence? It wasn't like I could let him go, so we now found ourselves in quite a quandary.

"You're obviously not a pup," I said quietly, preferring to stave off an attack of some sort. "Change back into your human form, and we'll discuss this without bloodshed."

It's not my intention to draw your attention away from the matter at hand, but we seem to have unexpected visitors.

"You, there!" a man's voice exclaimed right as the focused beam of a flashlight cut through the trees. "Did you not see the sign posted near the road? It's not safe for you—"

The beast before me took off, causing me to instantly lift my hands in order to use my ability to stop it from escaping. I barely caught myself in time before exposing the existence of werewolves to the park ranger who'd appeared out of nowhere.

"Hank!" the park ranger exclaimed, swinging his flashlight a little too late to catch sight of the beast. "Hank, I saw something run into the—"

Oh, dear.

"A deer," I replied loudly, forcing my tone to remain friendly when what I really wanted to do was yell at the park ranger for interfering with what possibly could have ended these murders. "Sir, it was nothing more than a deer."

That's not exactly what I meant by my exclamation, but you made a good recovery, dear hexed one.

I'd found throughout my life that sometimes a planted seed was more believable than a sudden appearance of an entire forest. This park ranger would be more likely to trust me that what I saw was nothing as outlandish as a wolf standing on two legs.

Gullible is the description I'd use, but we can go with your choice of words, if that makes you happy.

No wonder both creatures had sniffed the air. They'd caught the scent of intruders coming from the east. Our spell for the immediate area of the RV had protected the beasts from getting a whiff of Knox and us, but that was the limited range of the protection ward. Had the incantation extended farther into the forest itself, the werewolves would have immediately known that something was wrong when their most powerful sense had suddenly gone dead...most likely coming to the conclusion that either magic was the culprit or that another predator was masking his or her scent.

Speaking of culprits, I'm relatively sure we didn't have a plan for coming up empty-handed.

"Are you sure, ma'am?" the park ranger asked, taking a step closer to me so that he could shine his flashlight down toward the ground looking for prints. Rain was due in a couple of days, but at the moment the ground was thankfully dry and covered with leaves to prevent any obvious type of footprints from being found. "I could have sworn..."

"He was a beautiful buck, maybe even a twelve-pointer."

"That must have been why the shadow appeared so tall," the park ranger assumed, his supposition playing into my description. I sighed in relief, but this missed opportunity meant we'd be here for at least a couple more days. "Ma'am, did you not see the sign posted near the road about the animal attacks? It's not safe to be out in this area."

If only he knew…

The park ranger mumbled something underneath his breath about how they should have closed all the campsites. I pasted a smile to my face and gestured toward the main area where the RV was parked so that I could reassure him we were, indeed, safe.

Safe is such a relative term while werewolves roam the area.

"I was just looking for some firewood," I replied, leaning down and picking up a broken piece of wood that was located near the trunk of the tree. "We're aware of what's been happening over the last few weeks, but we're just passing through in our RV. It's after two o'clock in the morning, and we started to have a problem with one of our tires. We thought it was best to fix it now so that we can be on our way in the morning."

Little does this park ranger know that we'll be having breakfast at the diner and talking with the locals. Mr. Cornelia might need to pry a balance weight off that tire come morning, but we have more important things to deal with…such as the driver who is currently speaking with a park ranger named Hank.

"…know better than to be out here this late at night, Noah. Were you seriously going to try and hunt down this wolf all on your own? Did you even stop to think that another attack could have happened out here tonight?"

Your victim is getting reprimanded by Park Ranger Hank, dear hexed one.

I could hear that for myself, and I was actually grateful for the distraction. The park ranger who I was standing next to gravitated toward the campsite. I followed by his side, relieved that his attention was on something else besides what he'd thought he'd seen running off into the woods.

I can no longer hear their presence. Although they did leave behind quite the stench, wouldn't you agree? Wet dog is not my preferred scent of cologne. I prefer tomcat.

Orwin had turned on the RV's overhead spotlights, giving the clearing enough lighting so that it was easy to view the small campsite we occupied. Knox was kneeling on the ground, appearing to have actually taken off one of the tires. Orwin made no qualms about watching the scene in front of him unfold between the second park ranger and the man I'd seen in my vision. As for Piper, she'd opened the door and held a couple bottles of water in her hands and feigning her concern about the unexpected confrontation.

You know, my sweet Piper could have been an actress. You have the situation handled from here on in, correct? It's quite chilly, and I'm in need of a spot of cream.

Now that Pearl had mentioned it, the temperature had dropped quite precipitously. I tossed the hunk of wood to the side when I realized that the park ranger's attention was no longer on me. He'd joined his partner, clearly wanting in on the lecture that was taking place.

"Noah, you know you shouldn't be out here. We've got this covered, and don't think for a second we don't know about Brady and his brother-in-law organizing a wolf hunt for tomorrow morning. Is that why you're out here? Did they send you early to scout the area? Are they planning to be out in the woods by daybreak?"

Seeing the man I'd witnessed in my head be mauled to death was rather odd, especially since he was alive and well. That nervous energy I'd sensed in my vision was still there, but it made sense given that he'd been caught attempting to do something against the official advice of the park rangers.

"Did you know that Tommy's body has already been cremated? His service is tomorrow afternoon, and the thing that killed him is still out there roaming around," Noah replied with more resignation than anger. He shoved his hands into the front pocket of his jeans and shook his head in frustration. "Tommy was Lisa's brother. She's devastated, and nothing I say or do can get her to stop crying at the mere mention of his name."

Lisa Sutter. Russell Thomas Sutter. The pieces of the puzzle began to fall into place. He had been one of the victims, but Piper hadn't been able to find a social media account for him on any of the platforms. Lisa had a Facebook and Instagram account, but she referred to her brother as Russ. There would have been no way of knowing that Russell Sutter went by his middle name of Tommy to his friends. In all likelihood, Lisa and their mother were the only ones who called the victim by his given name.

Well, it seems that I'm not going to get that spot of warm cream anytime soon. I'm tired of being invisible. I'm making an appearance.

"Hey," I muttered, joining Orwin next to the RV. He was feigning using a rag to wipe his hands, while Knox continued to put back the tire he'd taken off. I made a mental note to have Orwin check the lug nuts to make sure they were replaced properly. As for Pearl, she came out from underneath the RV and settled next to Piper. "I was face to face with one of the werewolves. I couldn't do a thing about it, though. The park ranger with the red hair came out of nowhere, so I had to let it go. Did you get a read on any of them?"

I was already aware of Orwin's answer, but I had to ask anyway.

"No. I'm too far away." Orwin frowned at the inconvenience. It wasn't like he would have had a reason to interrupt their conversation. That would most likely cause undue attention on us, especially when we would be sticking around for a few days after I'd already mentioned we were just passing through. "I could always just ask if everything is all right."

Orwin had picked up on my thoughts, and I had to wonder if he was doing the same to Knox. Had I made a mistake letting him join us on this case?

"No, Emeric can definitely help us."

"Nice to know I can come in handy," Knox said wryly without looking up from his task. "Just so you know, that kid over there is scared. I can smell his fear from here."

Mr. Noah certainly looks pale in this lighting, does he not?

"…go on home." Park Ranger Hank, as Pearl had already referred to him as, slapped Noah on the shoulder a couple of times in sorrow. "Spend the day with Lisa. You might as well tell Brady that no one is going to be allowed to traipse around these woods tomorrow morning. Tommy's funeral service is in the afternoon, and his family members should be there to comfort the rest of the family."

Noah had on a thick flannel jacket, but it was un-zipped in the front showing a black t-shirt. It was a comfort to know that he was in the same clothes as what I'd envisioned. Those types of small details were essential and had cost someone their life in one of our earlier cases. Now, it was something I always checked before being rest assured that the danger had passed.

Unfortunately, it was too late for Orwin to figure out a way to get closer to Noah to get a read on the man's thoughts. Knox had called him a kid, but Noah was in his mid-twenties, and he was now getting in his vehicle and backing up in order to pull out.

"With everything going on, I didn't get a chance to introduce myself," the park ranger said as he closed the distance between us. Park Ranger Hank continued to monitor Noah's brake lights, more concerned with the fact that some of the locals were feeling it necessary to take matters into their own hands. "My name is Shane Harper, and I'm one of the local park rangers in the area. We've got a post in town. As I'm sure you just overheard, the town's a bit on edge after some wild animal attacks taking place over the last two months."

And rightly so. It is rather sad that these humans don't know what is happening in their own backyard.

"We heard about what happened when we stopped in at the gas station about twenty miles back," I replied, stepping forward and shaking hands with Shane. Orwin and Piper did the same, while Knox took the rag from Orwin in order to wipe his hands. "As soon as we're done changing the tire on the RV, we'll head inside. It wasn't our intention to stay outside for too long."

I could only hope that Shane forgot my reasoning for being in the woods.

It was a good idea at the time, Miss Lilura.

"Do you need any help?" Shane offered, peering around Orwin and Knox to see that they already had things under control.

That's an interesting question I've asked Mr. Cornelia numerous times myself. Of course, I'm usually referring to his mental health.

"We're good, but we appreciate the offer," Knox replied with a nod of his head. Orwin was busy shooting a glare Pearl's way, but he managed a smile in agreement with Knox's reply. "I couldn't help but overhear. A lone wolf attacking humans? That doesn't happen too often. Is he sick or hurt?"

"Last time something like this took place was close to five years ago," Hank chimed in, apparently satisfied that Noah had exited the campsite. He pulled his flashlight out of his utility belt as he joined Shane. "I have to wonder if it's the same wolf. We never did capture the elusive fellow last time. Three deaths, though, in the last eight weeks. Shame. Real shame."

I'd assume three deaths would get national attention, wouldn't you?

Pearl made a good point. Orwin's search parameters had included local news, which was how he was able to locate this minuscule town on a map, along with obscure names of the two campsites.

"Listen, we're working the night shift." Shane made eye contact with each and every one of us, not blinking an eye when he saw Pearl. I'm sure park rangers have seen stranger things at campsites than a cat. "We'll check on you every now and then, but please take precautions. I'd also make sure your house pet is secure inside at all times. This is no place for a domesticated animal."

He's human. I'll try not to take offense over the term house pet.

After another few words of caution, Hank and Shane began to walk toward the back of the campsite. They must have been monitoring that specific area for a while before hearing Orwin and Knox kibitz about the tire. They were diligent in their job to check it out, and it made me wonder how two more murders had taken place after the first one was declared an animal attack.

"Well?" I asked Orwin, knowing full well he'd caught every thought that had passed through Shane and Hank's minds as they'd stood in front of us. "Anything we should be aware of?"

"Nada." Orwin sighed and leaned back against the RV, crossing his arms as he watched the two men fade into the shadows. "Hank was worried that Noah and the other Buchanans were going to give them trouble come morning, and Shane thought it was odd that Pearl was here. Oh, and he was still thinking about the deer you said ran into the woods and if maybe it was a sixteen-point rack given how tall the shadow looked as it ran off."

"Not that your ability doesn't come in handy, but are you sure they didn't know what we are and what we're capable of?" Knox inquired quietly, seemingly not wanting to offend anyone with the fact that he'd been able to outsmart us back in Bedford. There was a lot that we needed to discuss, but I was too tired after driving eighteen hours and basically confronting a werewolf to do it now. His golden gaze met mine without regret before switching his focus to Orwin. "I will say that it wasn't always easy keeping my thoughts clear in your presence. In all honesty, it got physically draining at times."

Is it just me or does Mr. Emeric have an accent?

He did, and it was definitely from the state of Washington.

"I can never be sure. Looking back at our previous encounters, your thoughts were rather one-dimensional. I never gave it much deliberation at the time. Now that I think about it, those park rangers had other random bits of information floating in the back of their consciousness. Hank was concerned about Noah being out here this late at night, and he's going to follow up with Brady to ensure that no one does anything foolish. Shane didn't seem as concerned, but I kept picking up his apprehension over an upcoming doctor's appointment."

Oh, dear. I'm not much of a fan of veterinarians, so I can understand Mr. Harper's trepidation.

"I hate to bring this up," Piper chimed in before handing the bottles of water she'd brought outside to Orwin and Knox. "We might have saved Noah's life tonight, but we didn't catch the perpetrator...in this case, werewolf...who seems to have gone rogue hunting humans."

Two, my sweet Piper. There were two werewolves closing in on our victim.

"I'm not so sure these creatures have gone rogue," I fessed up warily, not realizing how I'd worded my opinion until I caught the arch of Knox's brow. I wasn't going to apologize for the fact that my previous encounters with the supernatural beasts hadn't ended on the best note. "Had the one I confronted been rogue, he would have wasted no time in attacking me. Trust me when I say he had complete control over his primal urges, which begs to question…why would he want to murder a twenty-something year old man? And was he the one responsible for the other killings?"

We had a win tonight, Miss Lilura. These remaining questions will be there to answer in the morning. Now, about that spot of warm cream…

Chapter Six

"ARE WE READY to head into town?" Piper asked as she stepped down from the RV's entrance. She was in the middle of putting on her brown peacock jacket, but stopped short of wrapping her scarf around her neck when she'd noticed the tension. "Um, I take it now is when we're having the *why didn't you tell us you were a werewolf* discussion?"

It was bound to happen sooner or later, my sweet. Either that or the hexed one over there was about to go find herself some silver bullets.

I'd gotten up early with every intention of finally finding out who Knox Emeric really was and why he'd been following us for the past several weeks. Apparently, I wasn't the only one with that grand idea. Orwin and Pearl had already been up and ready to take a go at him. To say that the two rarely agreed on anything would be an understatement, so seeing them both standing side by side near the door of the RV had been somewhat of a shock.

Stranger things have happened than me seeing eye to eye

with Mr. Cornelia, dear hexed one. Such as we both agree you need to laugh a bit more.

"Bad timing, Pearl," Orwin muttered with a shake of his head. "Bad timing."

The morning chill hadn't dissipated, and it was a fair bet that it wouldn't burn off until ten or later, given the time of year. The woods were eerily quiet, as was usual with predators lurking about. In fact, the air around us was so still that it was easy to hear the smaller wildlife run across the fallen dead leaves that covered the ground. Orwin had cast a protective ward around the campsite to alert us should anyone or anything larger than a small doe come within twenty feet of the RV, but that shouldn't have put us in a bubble. It was as if the heavy silence was a precursor of thing to come.

Bad timing, Mr. Cornelia? We're hunting down a cure for a hex given by the Lich Queen herself while saving as many lives as we can in the process. We're lucky we have time to go to the loo. This predicament—yes, I said predicament, dear hexed one—shows us we need to make the best of what time we are given. There are no guarantees.

Orwin pushed up his black-rimmed glasses before pinching the bridge of his nose in the utter hopelessness of corralling Pearl or her opinions. Then again, no one was able to hold back the sleek white familiar from giving her opinion in the best of situations—just as no one was going to be able to interrupt this fact-finding mission that was about to come to an end once and for all.

I turned to face Knox, who was leaning against the side of my Jeep, despite numerous other places he could choose to stand.

"I asked you before who you were, and you purposefully evaded the question by threatening Piper and her family with outing them publicly with the fact that they are witches," I pointed out to Knox, my previous anger coming to the forefront. Orwin and Pearl could continue to debate on how to best use one's time, but I was going to use mine by getting to the truth. "As one supernatural being to another, that's pretty low."

I agree with that assessment, dear hexed one. Not the time to debate, of course, but regarding the unwritten rules of loyalty. If that is now followed, mutually assured destruction would prevail within the supernatural realm. He broke that rule.

I'm sure Pearl did agree with my second assessment, considering that she'd used the term *eliminate* in her response to such a discovery back in Bedford. She'd been ready to dispose of Knox's body upon learning what he'd done two weeks ago. Had he not disappeared of his own volition, I'm relatively sure she would have followed through with it.

"His body? I distinctly recall that Pearl wanted to find a place to dispose of his skull," Orwin murmured, not helping our current situation. He shrugged as if he'd given me valuable information, while Piper scooped Pearl up just in case she still harbored some resentment. "Oh, that allergy-inducing furball absolutely harbors resentment."

You know nothing of the sort, Mr. Cornelia. Hush.

"I did not threaten Piper or her family," Knox amended carefully, still leaning against my Jeep that Orwin and I had already unhooked from the RV. We would use the Jeep to go into town after getting any useful information from Knox…most importantly, who he was and what he wanted with us. "I pointed out that it was a distinct possibility the woman who'd died in that café had known about the Allifair family secret. I was just trying to help your little investigation along."

"You didn't, in case you were wondering." I realize that came out a little harsh, but the man had been following us for way too long. It was time for some answers. "What do you know about us, and why are you following our merry little band, Emeric?"

I'd used his surname so as to cut the familiarity that seemed to have grown over night. He wasn't part of our team, but he was essentially somewhat quasi-related to the very creatures we were hunting down today.

"You want the truth? Fine. I know you were cursed by Ammeline Letty Romilda, just as I was back in Washington."

Well, that is quite a shock. Seeing as Mr. Emeric cannot hear me, is someone going to speak or are we just going to stand around here all day with our mouths hanging open?

Pearl had a point, considering at least a minute had passed since anyone had uttered a word after Knox's bombshell. I needed to take a seat after hearing that shocking disclosure, so I shooed Knox to the side and opened my passenger side door. Once I was settled in the seat with my boots on the running board, I was feeling composed enough to address his declaration.

"You were cursed? By Ammeline? By the Queen Lich herself?"

"Now you're sounding like my echo," Piper said with a wry smile, reminding me of her reaction upon discovering my own predicament. She'd set Pearl down after Knox's bombshell before she began to pull on her gloves, reminding me that my own hands were quite cold. I wasn't so sure the reaction was due to the weather, though. "Knox, do you get visions of death? The same ones as Lou? Is that why you've been at two of the crime scenes?"

Oh, now you agree it's a predicament, dear hexed one?

This could change everything. I'd never considered that there were others out in the world like me. How many were there, and could we band together to destroy the evil power welded by the Queen Lich?

Destroy? It appears I'm not the only spiteful one in the group. Fire up the stakes, and I'm not referring to breakfast meats.

Piper hushed her familiar while keeping her blue eyes trained on Knox. She was coming into her own as a huntress, but she hadn't lost an ounce of her kindness or innocence.

"Knox, we can help you. You aren't alone."

My sweet Piper, let's hear what the mangy-haired dog—I mean, werewolf has to say.

"It's not like that. I don't foresee death or people's murders." Knox ran a hand over his five o'clock shadow, as if he were trying to carefully compose his words. I'm not sure why, considering he'd already dropped a heck of a bombshell…unless there was more. Maybe we should have waited to have this conversation after breakfast, because I could definitely use some coffee right about now. "I was out hiking around four months ago when I stumbled across a cave deep in the woods. I'd been in hundreds just like it, so I didn't even think twice about checking this one out. Caves can come in handy as an improvised shelter during inclement weather."

Mutts have a tendency to stick their noses into any hole in the ground, you know.

I caught Orwin's frown at Pearl's opinion of werewolves.

"She said mutts, but I'm pretty sure she meant men," Orwin pointed out, widening his stance and crossing his arms in irritation. "Sorry, Knox. Bad habit. Continue."

"What happened after you entered the cave?" Piper asked gently, casting me a worried glance. It was then I realized I hadn't said much since Knox had made his announcement. It was true that I was still digesting the news, but maybe I was still a bit too hesitant to believe that I wasn't the only cursed supernatural being in the world. "Was Ammeline inside?"

I had felt the weight of Knox's golden gaze, but I wasn't ready to admit that I believed him. Once again, I couldn't help but think that this could change everything. Sun Tzu was wise when he'd said there was power in numbers.

"Yes."

We all waited for Knox to expand on that one word reply, but the muscle alongside his jawline became taut as I'm sure the unwelcome memories of that encounter washed over him.

I don't mean to come across as indifferent or callous, but we are on a somewhat hectic schedule here.

"Knox, what did you see?" Piper prodded, her tone barely a whisper as if she was afraid of what his answer would entail.

"I'm not sure exactly," Knox replied after a while. He shook his head slowly as he chose his words carefully. Another moment passed when it was clear he was still grappling with what had transpired in the cave. I could literally see the exact moment when he covered up his vulnerability and became the man he'd most likely been in the past—guarded. "I'm a former active duty military operator. I worked at a high-end consulting firm for private security systems and consulting, and I had a pretty good life laid out in front of me. I certainly wasn't prepared for what I encountered in that cave, and it took close to a week before I figured out how to change back into my human form. That was after it took two days to walk upright and regain my previous mental abilities. Prior to then, I was an animal in almost all respects."

I give Mr. Emeric his due. Most humans in that situation wouldn't have had the strength to learn the change on their own without guidance, let alone keep their sanity.

I cleared my throat, wanting to ask so many questions that I didn't know where to start. It was rare I was caught off guard like this, but here we were—two cursed individuals with the same goal of finding a cure to two vile hexes that had all but ruined our lives. I wasn't alone anymore. Neither was he.

You were never alone, dear hexed one.

Chapter Seven

"HE'S TELLING THE truth, Lou." Orwin appeared somewhat apologetic that he'd read Knox's thoughts, but our resident werewolf didn't seem offended in the least. "Sorry. Bad habit."

Most likely, Knox's lack of offense was due to his knowledge of our collective abilities. He'd mentioned he was former military. That alone told me that he was cautious, planned meticulously, and got the layout of the land before venturing too far if given the opportunity.

"Well, except the cave," Orwin pointed out, holding up his hand once again in apology when Knox arched an eyebrow. "Emeric, how did you even know about Lou, her hex, and what we are?"

"I was in that cave for over a week. I'm not afraid to admit that I was terrified of what I'd become, and I came to a lot of conclusions in those seven days. The cave...let's just say it was filled with fear and a wretched stench that I'll never forget." Knox allowed a bit of tension to escape his shoulders, and he leaned against the back passenger door of my Jeep. The cold morning air didn't seem to bother him in the least, but now I understood the reason why. "Once I changed back into human form, I didn't leave right away. I couldn't. I wasn't really me, and I was afraid someone would notice. Either that, or I wouldn't be in control of myself. How could I explain something I didn't understand myself? So, I spent another three agonizing days forcing the change. I did that until I was confident it wouldn't happen unexpectedly around innocent people."

I might have been too hasty with my original assessment. This particular werewolf has strong principles, my sweet Piper.

"By the time I was done, there was one thing in-grained in me that I will forever remember—that horrific stench." Knox's expression was one of distaste, but that didn't stop him from continuing. "I made my way home, knowing that my life had changed and that nothing would ever be the same until I hunted down the vile being responsible. I sold my half of the partnership to my business colleague, sublet my apartment to a trusted friend, and explained to my family and friends that I needed time to myself…that I was going to do a bit of traveling and soul-searching. My mother believes that I'm doing some contracting work for the Department of Defense, while several others believe I'm suffering from PTSD. I make sure to stay in touch once a week so they don't call the authorities on me or try to track me down for some type of intervention."

And he cares for his family. My respect for him is growing, dear hexed one.

Knox rubbed his five o'clock shadow. It was as if he was contemplating how much to share with us. I wanted to reassure him that nothing at this point was off limits. The slightest detail could be helpful to our mutual cause of taking down Ammeline, and we needed to be aware of everything possible. It didn't escape me that I was going to have to reciprocate. If that meant ridding me of this hex, I'd tell Knox anything and everything he needed to know.

"Once I'd packed what I needed, I set out to find the creature who was responsible for what I'd become…and tracking that wretched stench led me straight to the campus of a fair-sized community college." Knox paused, giving us time to grasp his meaning. Of course, it didn't take long. He'd been there that fateful morning when I'd been hexed by the Queen Lich herself. "I wasn't sure what I'd seen between you and the Lich, but I could hear every word you and Orwin exchanged after your run-in with Ammeline."

There is something to be said for combining our forces, my valued colleagues.

I do recall taking in my surroundings and spotting Orwin standing off to the side after my unfortunate encounter with Ammeline. It hadn't been that difficult to ascertain his obvious familiarity with the arcane language she'd used from his shaken expression. His mouth had been hanging open in shock at what he'd just witnessed.

Having a spectator who could provide some type of reassurance that I hadn't just met a very powerful supernatural being, I'd instantly gone to him. Of course, he'd confirmed the opposite—I had just experienced a run-in with an immortal.

The resulting conversation would have indeed given a great deal of information to anyone who might have been listening in…say from a distance that a werewolf could overhear with their superior hearing.

There was no argument that werewolves were apex predators. They combined their extraordinary senses of vision, smell, and hearing to extend their awareness of their surroundings. They could easily listen to the fear and panic that laced an individual's words, sniff those same indicators, and observe the tremors as the blood pumped through their prey's veins at an accelerated rate.

Their hearing distance on its own is quite remarkable, you know. They can virtually paint a three-dimensional picture of an unseen area with that sense alone. Did you know that werewolves can hear a heartbeat thump against a chest like a bass drum from fifty yards away? It's truly astonishing.

"You found out that we weren't human," Orwin said, presuming aloud what we'd already determined. He pushed up his glasses and ran a hand through his dark hair before getting to the heart of the matter. "You've been following us in hopes that we can lead you to

Ammeline again. Did she realize you were tracking her and cover her scent?"

"Something like that. And yes, my original plan was to have you lead me to her. That changed over the last few months after coming to the conclusion you're not looking for that...Lich," Knox amended with a wry smile. I didn't like that he'd been tracking our every move for months. Who else had been able to do the same? I made a mental note to speak with Orwin about some type of ward, but even I realized the impossibility of such a ubiquitous incantation. It wasn't like we could all put ourselves into a bubble and pretend the outside world didn't exist. "You're looking for a cure, and that works for me. We can either work together or go our separate ways with the same objective in mind. All that's going to do is take more effort on both our parts, so I suggest some sort of understanding or pact."

Have we made a decision, valued colleagues? Are we bringing Mr. Emeric into the fold?

I had to ponder on such a momentous decision, but it certainly seemed as if that was the best choice. He brought a lot of unique strengths to the table. With that said, I had no doubt that should Knox ever find a cure to his own hex, he'd never give up his pursuit of finding Ammeline Letty Romilda and holding her accountable.

I'd say that qualifies you as two peas in a pod, wouldn't you?

"Let me give it some thought." I vacated the passenger seat and stood next to the door, wanting this current case we were working over and done with so that I could give my full attention to this monumental decision. Who would have thought we'd hook up with a werewolf on this quest? I certainly hadn't, and there were good reasons for that—ones that were generally very sharp and had an overt advantage come the full moon. These particular lycanthropes had multiplied that advantage by mastering the ability to change at will. "In the meantime, let's head into town. It's obvious that the park rangers stopped the Buchanan family from their hunt of vengeance or else we would have seen or heard something by now."

I feel empathy for that family.

We all did, but a life that was entwined with the Buchanans had been saved last night. That had to count for something in the balance.

"There are two park rangers at the turnoff to the secondary road off the main highway," Knox offered, tapping his ear. He seemed completely fine with my decision to postpone our discussion until later. "The shift change happened around forty-five minutes ago. I'm going to skip the diner for a stroll around the woods instead. I'm picking up a scent north of here that tells me there's a pack's lair within range. I'll scope out the area to see what we're dealing with and then meet you back here this afternoon."

Knox turned on his boots and walked to his Land

Rover to open the back. I almost let him go without another word, but then thought better of it. Orwin and Piper proceeded to get into the Jeep while I followed Knox, feeling compelled to share something with him.

"Knox."

He turned to face me after having pulled out a large and what looked to be a very well-equipped backpack. Now that I had his full attention, I couldn't quite recall what I'd wanted to say.

"Neither one of us did anything to deserve this...suffering," Knox replied quietly, filling the void. He'd gotten a faraway look in his golden eyes, telling me he'd briefly had a visit with his past. "I'll rephrase that. I've certainly done things in my life that may or may not have been the right decision. I did my duty, and I don't regret a day I served defending our freedom. But Ammeline Letty Romilda doesn't get to be my judge and jury, and I'm banking the same goes for you."

I slowly nodded my agreement, still needing some time to accept everything I'd heard this morning. Chalk it up to the lack of caffeine or the shock of discovering that I wasn't the only cursed supernatural being in existence. Either way, it was a relief to know I wasn't alone anymore.

"I'm sorry, Knox. I'm sorry that you had your life, family, and friends stolen from you." I should have said more, maybe even given him my own story of how I'd come to be in this position. It was clear he knew the basics, but he didn't know the emotional and mental toll it had taken on me. Unfortunately, now wasn't the time with a rogue werewolf or two roaming around these woods. Even more unfortunate was knowing we'd have plenty of time in the days ahead, because whatever cure was out there wasn't even remotely close to being found. "Be safe out there. They have you outnumbered."

You handled that well, dear hexed one.

"Pearl, we really need to talk about privacy," I muttered, inhaling deeply as I turned around and walked to the driver's side of the Jeep. The red paint clearly needed a wash, but it would have to wait until this case was over. "I wonder if you shouldn't go with Knox. If he can grab the scent of a pack, they most certainly would have done the same with him. Our ward has most likely worn off, and he can't guarantee that he'll always be downwind of his adversaries."

Oh, that was taken care of before you woke up this morning. Mr. Knox now has a ward around him, preventing any adversary from gaining the upper hand by detecting his scent.

Orwin and I had gotten so used to handling things on our own that it was rather difficult to remember we had help in the form of another witch. Piper might be a healer, but she was a gem when it came to casting spells off the cuff.

That she is, Miss Lilura.

"Hey, I want to run something by the two of you," I exclaimed after opening the driver's side door. I leaned in, but I didn't take my place behind the wheel just yet. "Noah was here because of the Buchanan family. We all agreed that the victims had friends in common due to the size of the town, but what if all the murders are somehow connected to the Buchanan family?"

"That's going to take some research." Orwin was sitting in the passenger seat, while Piper had hopped into the back. He sneezed the moment Pearl had jumped into the vehicle, not seeing the direction I was taking with this conversation. "Are there tissues in here?"

You wouldn't have the need for tissues if you'd allow Piper to utilize her gift.

"Not a chance." Orwin used his thumb to indicate Knox's location. "In case you missed this morning's briefing, that man turns into a massive beast. A big mangy, hairy creature. That's exactly what happens when one doesn't have a protective ward around oneself to prevent such magic, and this particular ward I concocted took months to cast with material spell components I no longer possess. No, thank you."

"He does have a point," I conceded with a half-smile, though there was nothing funny about our situation.

There is such a thing as paranoia. We wouldn't do such an intricate spell without the proper reinforcements.

"Not happening," Orwin protested, holding up his hands in response to Piper tossing a small packet of tissues from the back seat. "Not in this lifetime."

Piper's inquisitive gaze landed on me. Knox had

already disappeared somewhere deep into the woods, walking at a brisk pace. Would his stroll in the forest land him on one of the Buchanan's extended family member's doorstep? It certainly wasn't out of the question.

"The victims did have friends in common, but I don't recall seeing a familial link between them," Piper said with a frown, reaching for her seat belt. "I guess we'll find out more once we get into town, though I'm not sure we'll get too much information from the diner. You know how small towns are about keeping to their own."

As well they should be, my sweet Piper. A tight-knit community is very important when it comes to protecting its citizens.

The answers did lie somewhere in town and with the Buchanan family, but that meant two different avenues of approach. There was definitely going to be a slight change in today's plans.

"Orwin?" I waited for him to look my way. When he met my gaze, he accepted his fate with an audible frustrated sigh. "I'm sorry, but as much as Piper has been beneficial in the research area, neither one of us compares to you and your programs. We'll head into town for a quick breakfast while you run the search. We'll bring you back something to eat. Besides, you hate when either one of us touches your machine, and you know it."

Does Mr. Cornelia know about the small coffee spill?

"The what?" Orwin asked, his thin black eyebrow rising above the rim of his glasses. "Lou, please tell me that you didn't—"

"Pearl is just ruffling your feathers." The sleek white familiar had already jumped over the console to get comfortable in the backseat. She'd do her invisible thing the closer we got to town, allowing her to slip in and out of places without anyone else being the wiser. "I didn't spill anything on your keyboard."

That you know of, Miss Lilura. Who is to say that my tail didn't bump into your cup when you weren't looking?

"Shhh," Piper hushed her familiar and cast a frown her way. "Be nice or no cream."

There were times it was difficult to make an executive decision that might prolong the investigation. Orwin's telepathic ability was undoubtedly vital in situations like these, but he had a gift when it came to technology. The only reason I was comfortable with keeping him at the campsite for a couple additional hours was that the victim's fate in my vision had already been changed.

"Piper and I will get the layout of the town, along with who we might need to speak with this afternoon in regard to the so-called animal attacks," I told Orwin, seeing Piper nodding in agreement. She'd released her seat belt and reached for the door handle so that she could switch seats and ride shotgun. "Once we have a list of names, we'll come back for you."

"Fine," Orwin said in somewhat of a grunt. He grabbed the handle and shouldered open the passenger side door with one request. "Don't forget to get me a breakfast burrito—mild salsa. Oh, I get a big lunch for this sacrifice, too. That's in addition to a new keyboard, if I find out that anyone spilled coffee on the one I have now."

"You're horrible," I muttered to Pearl, making myself comfortable behind the steering wheel while Piper switched seats. "You realize that you're fifty-one percent of the cause for his paranoia."

I've taken it upon myself to lighten the state of disposition around here. If it's at Mr. Cornelia's expense, then so be it. He's more than capable of handling the load.

"Pearl, did you tell her the knock-knock joke that we heard a few weeks ago?"

I put the Jeep in reverse, carefully maneuvering the vehicle until we were finally on our way back toward the main road. Was it too much to hope that the trip into town would discourage them from visiting jokeville?

Knock-knock, Miss Lilura.

Chapter Eight

"DOES FOUR-HUNDRED AND three residents even make up a town? Wouldn't it be considered a village?" Piper asked quietly as she reached for the maple syrup. We'd ended up having to wait a good fifteen minutes for a table to open up, but that was to our advantage. We were able to stand near the entrance, study the patrons, and listen to idle chatter. It seemed that this diner was the place to be on a Saturday morning. "I'm not even sure it constitutes as a village."

According to the standard definitions, this place is just large enough to constitute a village. Anything less than five hundred residents is usually considered a hamlet, and then there's this little issue—I heard the mayor is currently enjoying his breakfast over at the far table.

Pearl had been invisible ever since we'd passed the gas station, but she'd been commenting on quite a lot since we'd walked into the diner. I wasn't sure what the significance of the mayor having breakfast in the diner had to do with a village or a hamlet being one or the other.

A village nor a hamlet has a mayor, dear hexed one. I

do believe Orwin has a set of encyclopedias loaded to your laptop back at camp if you'd care to schedule in some study time. Then, of course, there's always Wikipedia, if he's actually reestablished his link to that old MilSat satellite and gotten us free highspeed internet again.

Besides a basic resource library, we had a grand collection of magical tomes in the RV, which meant Pearl was just being derisive. She'd been on this earth for over two thousand years, if not longer. The numerous and various facts she'd picked up along the way were astronomical. In situations like this, her wisdom was priceless…though I could do without the witty commentary.

I do so love a backward compliment. And wit is good for the soul, my dear.

The town itself was basically a stretch of red brick buildings lining either side of the road for three or four blocks, though it was obvious some restoration had been done. I'm sure the place had an appealingly quaint vibe to it during the spring and summer months when the flowerbeds had vibrant colored blooms and the small trees planted out front had full branches.

The overcast day did nothing but conceal what was most likely a charming spot on the map. Their fall display was nice enough as the pumpkins and gourds were plentiful, but spring was definitely the season to explore this place. As for the pumpkins, it wouldn't surprise me if we ended up having an additional knick-knack in the RV by the time we pulled out of this town.

The diner itself appeared as if we'd been thrown back to the late fifties or early sixties. There were black and white pictures of Elvis and Marilyn Monroe hanging on the wall, and each table and booth had those old replica jukeboxes with flip file selections for the darkened Wurlitzer that stood in the corner. I'm not sure even it worked anymore. The checkerboard floor contained chips in the tiles, the red vinyl chairs had faded to a deep pink, and the long hardwood counter had to be the same one installed at the time the diner had been built. One had to wonder how many coats of varnish had been slapped onto it over the years.

"It's probably a good thing we left Orwin behind." I sipped my coffee as I leisurely scanned the faces of all the patrons, noticing that some were staring back at me with interest and no small measure of caution. "He doesn't do too well in crowded, tight places like these. Truthfully, I don't know how he can listen to so many people at once, and this place would no doubt have been a massive overload of information."

There are no witches or warlocks present, if that helps. Although I do catch a lingering whiff of wet dog, which is not unexpected given that we're in their territory. I'm sure they've been here at some point.

For Pearl, I'm sure the lack of supernatural beings was a relief. Unfortunately, an individual didn't need to be supernatural for Orwin to pick up on his or her thoughts. I'm not sure why I thought about Knox, but the heavy aroma of grease hanging in the air probably would have irritated his senses, as well.

I wonder if Orwin would be able to utilize his ability with an alien life form. That is something we must give more thought to before driving to Nevada.

It was a good thing I had swallowed the sip of my coffee I'd been savoring or otherwise I would have inhaled the hot beverage down the wrong tube. I had not expected Pearl to give such an overt endorsement about Area 51.

Was that a chuckle I heard from you, dear hexed one?

I refrained from answering when Piper gestured with a fork in her right hand that I'd want to listen to the patrons at the table to our right. After all, we were here for the case.

Eavesdropping is very rude, but we must do what we are required to do. Please excuse me while I make the rounds, and we'll revisit what you do and don't find humorous at another time.

I wish Pearl would get off this kick of making me a bit more lighthearted. I had a fun side. I did. It had just been temporarily hidden underneath the massive weight of a hex cast by an infamous Lich Queen.

"...heard that he and his brother-in-law were told to go home by the park rangers. I can't imagine how difficult this is for Evelyn. Do you know that Nelson went ahead and cremated Tommy's body before she could see him? Of course, he had to do the same with the others. I don't know how the man can do his job and still sleep at night."

Nelson? Piper mouthed the name before taking a bite of her pancakes. I needed to listen a little more to understand who the players were in this town, so I picked at the blueberry muffin I'd ordered. I'd never been a big fan of breakfast. Coffee usually did the trick, but I didn't want to stand out in this small café. Well, any more than I already was, given that I was a complete stranger amongst the locals.

"I heard it was Benji who had Nelson carry through with Tommy's wishes for cremation. Besides, Evelyn shouldn't have that image in her head for the rest of her life," the other woman said, garnering nods from the other couple at her table. "I can't imagine losing one of my children, and in such a horrible fashion, too. Torn apart like that."

"I know for a fact that it *wasn't* Benji who made that request," her husband replied, the only one in disagreement. He leaned forward so that his voice didn't carry too far. "I spoke to him yesterday, and he mentioned that Brady must have talked to Nelson. You know how protective Brady is of Evelyn, being the big brother and all. I guess it doesn't matter much now. The service is this afternoon, and that boy will be laid to rest, proper like."

If I followed the conversation correctly, Nelson had to be the mortician at the funeral home. Benji was no doubt Brady Buchanan's brother-in-law, and Evelyn was

Brady's sister. Tommy, of course, had been the third the victim. I'd seen firsthand what a mauling looked like in the aftermath, and Brady had done right by his sister with insisting she not have that visual of her son in her head for all time.

"...poor Lisa. I heard she doesn't even want to attend today's service. She was so close to her brother. Did you know that Noah went out to the campsite last night with a rifle? Brady and Benji were fit to be tied when they found out that—"

"More coffee?" the waitress asked, jarring my attention away from the very interesting conversation.

Brady hadn't sent Noah to scout the woods last night?

Noah hadn't struck me as the type to do something so foolish. Given the fear that Knox had sensed and the nervous tics the young man had been displaying, I never would have guessed he'd taken it upon himself to hunt a wild animal in the middle of the night. Was his love for Lisa Sutter so strong that he felt the need to avenge her brother by himself?

"You gals passing through?" the waitress asked after I'd set down my half-empty mug on the table with an appreciative nod. She was a middle-aged strawberry blonde whose nametag read *Janet*. She didn't seem one bit fazed by the number of patrons in attendance. That alone told me that she had years of experience dealing with this crowd, and that skill had been learned in this very diner. She could be a wealth of information. "Or do you have a relative in town?"

"Oh, we're just passing through after we take a few days' rest," I replied with a smile, noticing that Piper was still trying to swallow the large bite of pancakes she'd taken a moment ago. Her blue eyes were trained on something near the window. I wanted to see what she was staring at, but I couldn't afford to have Janet think we weren't friendly. "We're on our way to visit a friend up north, but it was so late when we stopped at the gas station last night that we decided to stay out at one of the campsites twenty miles to the east."

Could you be any less conspicuous, Miss Lilura? We were never going to stay under the radar being strangers and all, but you did you have to blow into the bullhorn?

Sure enough, I'd garnered everyone's attention. And I mean everyone.

Piper ever so slowly lowered her fork until the metal audibly clinked against the plate, her focus still somewhere across the diner. The couple who had been sitting to the right of us had trouble closing their mouths at my announcement, but that's exactly what I'd wanted…to have the conversation veer toward the attacks.

Now might not have been such a great time to broadcast our arrival.

Pearl's warning told me that someone—most likely the individual who'd caught Piper's attention—was in the diner hanging on to our every word.

Yes. A werewolf, to be precise.

"Honey, you might want to reconsider staying out of that area," Janet said cautiously before pouring more coffee into my mug. There was a slight tremor in her task. "There have been some bad animal attacks recently. Three deaths, and one of them our own."

I cleared my throat, hoping that Pearl would point me in the right direction. Piper was now staring at a woman who'd apparently taken offense at Janet's approach of sharing the town's private business with complete strangers.

A booth near the display window. I thought the lingering wet dog scent was left over from a previous visit. Upon closer inspection, the older gentleman who is seated by himself uses cigarette smoke to cover up his stench. That was harsh, wasn't it? I do so apologize. It's fair to say that he can't stand my pleasant fragrance, either, though he hasn't indicated that he's aware of my presence. It makes me think no one else in this diner knows of his secret.

"Clyde, Mason, and Tommy were all a part of this town," the offended woman stressed at a nearby table, clearly not liking that only Tommy was getting attention. From the research that Orwin and Piper had done on the animal attacks, two of the victims had been from the rural area around here but not as deep-rooted in the community as Tommy. "Just because Clyde and Mason's families moved away doesn't mean we think of them any differently. Poor Nelson had to contact the families to pick up their sons' ashes. If you recall, Nelson went to school with Clyde's father not so many years ago."

I picked up my coffee and leaned back in my chair, hoping to be able to observe the older gentleman Pearl had outed while listening closely to what Janet and the other woman were saying. Piper was wiping her mouth with a napkin, carefully watching things unfold.

He doesn't seem the least bit fazed by this conversation. I find that quite interesting.

"I didn't mean anything by that, Brenda," Janet tried to smooth over, but Brenda's expression all but said the slight wouldn't be forgotten. The waitress turned back to our table, but I was scanning the patrons to try and find the reason for Piper and Pearl's concern. "Anyway, I'd suggest for you two to clear out of the area. I'm surprised the park rangers even allowed you to camp there last night."

"We spoke with two rangers last night, Hank and Shane. They did warn us to be careful in the area, but we were having a bit of tire trouble on the RV. I'm sure their indifference to us camping overnight was due to us being able to sleep inside." Camping in a tent versus an extremely large vehicle were two very different things. Brenda's husband was blocking my view, but Piper's attention was once more on the werewolf in question. "The park rangers were very kind and took the time to explain what has been taking place around here, and we are so very sorry to hear about your loss."

Piper nudged me under the table with her shoe, but it wasn't like I could stand up from my seat without looking conspicuous.

"We appreciate your sympathy," Janet said, though her frown was still in place. "Still, you'd best be careful while you're out at the campsite. Tommy was a very experienced camper, so no one expected to find him…"

Janet's voice trailed off when another wave of silence filled the diner and two men walked inside. Sure enough, I recognized Benji Sutter from one of the pictures Piper had found on Lisa Sutter's social media. The man he was with seemed a bit protective, so I figured it was safe to say that the taller man was none other than Brady Buchanan.

Well, he doesn't look very friendly, now does he?

Mr. Sutter was clearly grieving while anger simmered within Mr. Buchanan's dark eyes. It was evident that he wasn't pleased he'd been turned away by the park rangers this morning. I'd seen his boisterous type before, and he'd undoubtedly come to the diner to make sure everyone was aware of his opinion regarding how this investigation was being run by law enforcement officials.

"…poor Benji," one of the women to our right whispered. "What is Brady thinking bringing his brother-in-law here the day he's got to bury his son? It's a travesty, is what it is."

You should know that Brady Buchanan isn't well liked around these parts. All bark and no bite, but it's enough of a growl to keep people at arm's length. I don't mean in the werewolf sense, either. That's reserved for the older gentleman about to pay his bill and leave.

Piper didn't nudge me this time, but she instead full on kicked my shin. It was a good thing my black leather boots went up to my knee. I scooted back in my chair, attempting to get a better look at this werewolf when what I really wanted to do was have a conversation with Brady Buchanan. Of course, I did a three sixty in my thinking when I finally got a good look at the man Pearl and Piper had been so focused on.

Oh, my sweet Piper. I did not know that, but it certainly explains why you look a bit disheveled upon such a discovery. I wasn't aware the two of you had already been introduced.

I was in denial to what Pearl was discussing with Piper, because it meant that we'd been snookered last night while gathering intel. But sure enough, the werewolf in question was none other than the older man who'd been behind the counter at the gas station— Jasper.

This will teach me to stay behind in the RV when on a scouting mission. Duly noted, dear hexed one. Shall I follow this beast and see where he leads us?

Chapter Nine

"DO YOU THINK Pearl is going to be okay?" Piper asked with concern as we finally exited the diner. The morning chill in the air had not dissipated, and there was still fog hugging the ground in low-lying areas. The temperature was finally capitulating to the late season. The overcast sky made it easier for me to take a quick scan of the sidewalk and street without the deficit of deep shadows, but I didn't notice anything or anyone out of the ordinary. "I mean, Jasper has to know Pearl is somewhere nearby just by her scent."

Jasper.

A werewolf.

Who would have thought the elderly man who'd appeared barely able to summon the energy to get off his stool last night was a werewolf? He'd all but told us that the campsite was safe enough. According to him, these attacks happened every five years or so. Was it some sort of ritual? Did the pack need to bring so many new members into the fold to keep the pack viable? Had he been setting us up to be just another snack or the first kill for their new initiate?

"Pearl can handle her own," I replied, fully convinced that the white sleek familiar could take on an entire pack of werewolves and come out without a smudge of dirt on her pristine fur. "Besides, she has the upper hand by remaining invisible even from a werewolf's superior vision. We'll use the time we have to go speak with Noah. Did you hear what that couple said about Brady or Benji not knowing of Noah's plans? Something with his story isn't sitting right with me."

Noah's life had been spared last night, and this was not the run of the mill murder mystery we usually ended up attempting to solve while investigating this type of case. We could leave right now and never look back.

It was clear that a pack of werewolves had made this town their home for quite some time, though not necessarily within the core residents. Knox had gone hunting himself and would most likely discover a den area where the pack had set up residence when in animal form.

The pack wouldn't want to risk being discovered by one of their own going rogue, so what were we missing? I'd already jumped to the conclusion that Jasper had set us up last night, but that seemed a bit far-fetched if you dug into it.

We could easily go on our way, knowing that the pack would most likely solve their problem with their members amongst themselves. We weren't the fixers of the supernatural world, yet I couldn't bring myself to drive away in search of a cure for my hex and leave these innocent folks at the mercy of a rogue werewolf...or as Pearl had stated last night, two werewolves.

That was the kicker.

The odds of two werewolves going rogue at the same time and then being allowed to remain in the area to make two more kills were practically nonexistent. So, what was going on around here that we were missing?

"I don't mean to put a damper on your plans, but how do you expect to question anyone in this town without them calling the local police? We're complete strangers with a cover story that only buys us a few hours before we are driving north to visit a so-called friend," Piper pointed out, shoving her hands in her coat pockets. We were now standing beside the Jeep. "I guess we can say that we're checking in on him after being present during the lecture he received from the park rangers. Really, no one in their right mind would believe that...especially these folks."

"We're going to need to change our story or leave."

I gave it some thought while I continued to scan the other people milling about. Some were window shopping, some were driving past with a purpose, and I could see a few vehicles parked outside the funeral home some ways down the street. It was a stark reminder that one of their own had died. Even though we had the best of intentions of finding the beast responsible, we would no doubt come across as unsympathetic to the town's citizens no matter what story we came up with in the end.

"Lou?" Piper murmured, nudging me in the arm with her elbow.

A quick glance back toward the diner revealed Noah. It appeared the Fates weren't dealing us a totally bad hand, although I still held a grudge with Clotho and Lachesis for the unforeseen run in with the Queen Lich. Clotho spun the thread of human fate, and Lachesis dispensed it. Fortunately, Atropos hadn't seen fit to cut her thread just yet. A little warning would have been nice, though. You know, the occasional omen.

"Noah?" My calling out to the lucky victim who was fortunate enough to still be able to draw air into his lungs had caught him by surprise. He was wearing a dark suit, much like the one Brady and Benji were sporting in the diner. Now that I thought about it, most of the residents had been dressed for the upcoming funeral service. "You were at the campsite last night with us, right? My name is Lou, and this is Piper."

I closed the distance between us, mindful that the patrons of the diner could see Noah talking to me. He'd probably be ambushed with questions about what we were discussing, but I was pretty good at maneuvering the conversation to be viewed as nothing but friendly banter through experience.

"Boy, those rangers were really strict about those

campsites, weren't they?" I pulled out my black leather gloves, making it seem that I wasn't going to keep him long. "We ended up staying overnight—in the RV, of course. It makes camping so easy. Our friend stayed behind at the campsite to take another look at the tire we've been having problems with, so Piper and I thought we'd come into town for a quick bite to eat that we didn't have to fix ourselves. I didn't get a chance to tell you last night how sorry I was to hear about your friend."

Noah seemed a bit unnerved that I was talking to him with such familiarity. His uncomfortable gaze kept darting between me, Piper, and those residents through the window of the diner.

"Uh, thanks," Noah replied, tapping his thumb against the fabric of his pant leg. He'd been doing the same when I'd seen him in my vision. "Tommy was my girlfriend's brother, so it's been a really tough week for all of us."

"We heard a little about the animal attacks while we were eating breakfast," I replied with a shake of my head. "I can't imagine what your community has gone through in these past few weeks. I completely understand why you would want to go into the woods to hunt down the thing responsible for such a travesty. Piper actually thought she saw an animal roaming back and forth along the edge of the woods today. Right, Piper?"

"Yes," Piper replied with a small clearing of her throat. She gave Noah a sympathetic smile, following up with a compassionate sentiment. "I'm sorry for your loss. I can understand why everyone in the vicinity would be on edge. I usually drink my coffee and watch the sunrise, but I was too nervous this morning after talking with those park rangers last night. Is that why you were up there last night? To try and find the wolf responsible?"

A flash of anger—the first emotion I'd seen from Noah besides fear—came and went quickly. As a matter of fact, I wasn't so sure I'd even read his body expression correctly. Again, I couldn't help but think we were missing something very important that was all but staring us in the face.

"I can't imagine going up to the campsite by myself, let alone at night," Piper said after Noah didn't respond right away. She made it seem as if she were giving him credit. She also recognized that we were missing something, especially after overhearing that Brady had nothing to do with Noah's impulsive decision. The family almost had two funerals to attend had last night not gone as planned. "You're very brave to have taken that kind of chance, Mr...."

Piper had worked the conversation to a point where she could garner Noah's last name. It would allow Orwin or her the ability to do a broader search on the internet, thereby giving them a chance to make the connection I believed was somehow linked to the Buchanans.

"Martin. Noah Martin." He seemed to have composed himself enough to recognize that he was sharing an awful lot with two strangers. He loosened his tie while narrowing his eyes to consider what motives we could possibly have by initiating this conversation. "I have a very busy day ahead of me, so I best be going. It sounds like you're about to do the same. I hope everything is good with that tire of yours. Drive safe now."

Noah didn't give either Piper or me a chance to speak as he quickly made his way into the diner, making a beeline for Brady Buchanan's table. The older man leaned forward almost immediately, anguish written on his features that couldn't be mistaken.

"If Brady didn't want Noah up at the campsite for a bit of early scouting, why would he make a decision to go out there by himself?" Piper asked warily before we both began to make our way back to the Jeep. It wasn't like we could continue to stand on the sidewalk and stare into the diner at what was virtually a bunch of strangers. "Do you think Lisa Sutter would have asked Noah to do something so reckless?"

"It's a possibility, but not likely. Did you see Noah tapping his thumb against his leg? That's not fear. That's agitation, and it makes me believe he knew exactly what he was hunting last night. Listen, let's head back to camp to see if Orwin was able to connect the other victims to the Buchanans. He's not going to be happy that the diner didn't have breakfast burritos. I hope he's okay with a Denver omelet." I pulled the Jeep keys out of my pocket, but I still couldn't shake off the feeling that

Noah was well aware of the supernatural. "Knox might have had the right idea about seeking out the pack. They have to know who is responsible and who among them is drawing attention to their kind."

"Do they, though?" Piper asked skeptically before reaching for the door handle. "We've already established that these animal attacks haven't become national news. If another attack never took place, all of the recent headlines would drift away with the exception of the loss these families have endured."

I pondered on Piper's outlook of the situation as I made my way around to the driver's side of the Jeep. We were covering the same old ground and getting nowhere. Something needed to break, because Noah Martin was only going to fester in his anger as the day wore on…and the balance between humans and the supernatural could be shifted should he be able to prove his theory on the recent murders.

Knock-knock.

Chapter Ten

PEARL AND I spent the twenty-three-minute drive back to the campsite bantering back and forth about the most appropriate time to materialize out of thin air. I absolutely refused to fall prey to a surprise heart attack, especially after surviving the initial shock of being cursed by the Queen Lich herself all because Pearl couldn't control her sense of drama.

I tried not to think about that fact that my survival had fallen prey to the presence of a prim and proper cat who thought etiquette was reserved for others. I'd even pointed out that good manners would never have allowed her to enter my private space without a bit of notice.

We'd finally made it to our destination, and I found it odd that the entrance to the park campsite—specifically area 4B—was no longer guarded by the park rangers. The threat hadn't technically dissipated, but the park rangers must have returned to their post. Had they been following orders? They did have jobs to do outside of discouraging illegal wolf hunts. After all, there were over forty-eight different campsites covered by the park service in this county alone.

I know what you're thinking, dear hexed one, but those men in uniform were not werewolves nor were they born of magic. They are mere humans, just as Mr. Cornelia indicated last night. The lycanthropes we detected yesterday evening, including Jasper, are all from the same species of wolves. They're all related in some fashion. It's interesting to note that the subspecies Emeric comes from is entirely different. A northwestern grey wolf isn't actually the same as a Canis Lupus Occidentalis. In fact—

"I've run into quite a few law enforcement agency officers in the last three months," I pointed out, trying to sidestep Pearl's odd comment about Knox. I maneuvered the Jeep slowly down the dirt path toward the campsite and tried to emphasize my insight instead. "How are three deaths by a wild animal not national news? What are we missing? This has got to be the most frustrating case I've worked in the last four months."

Very good question, and one I'm guessing has more to do with the reporting either by the park rangers, the police, or the mortician. I'm sure there are a number of people involved with the official paperwork. Maybe they are downplaying the involvement of wolves intentionally.

"Or all of them are involved," Piper interjected with a shrug. "Ever since we walked into the gas station last night, we've all sensed something was off about this town. Now we know for a fact that Jasper is a werewolf, so it's a sure bet that there are others in this town who are as well."

I did get a whiff of wet dog smell hanging in the air when I exited the funeral home. The town is covered with it, and the damp season only enhances the scent.

"You know, we've been so busy looking for a connection between the victims," Piper pondered, reaching for the door handle before I could even bring the Jeep to a stop, "that we never considered they'd purposefully kept specific information out of their social media lives. That's it! What we need to do is look for the discrepancies."

Piper was out of the Jeep the moment I hit the brakes and well before I could respond, leaving me, Pearl, and Orwin's omelet behind to take a moment to ourselves.

So, this is what it's like to feel like a third wheel.

"If you're the third, then I'm the fourth," I muttered as I shifted the gear into park. A quick scan of the woods revealed nothing was amiss. Was Knox back from his scouting trip and inside the RV with Orwin? If so, it was a sure bet that he'd doubled up on his allergy medicine. "I've been meaning to tell you that you were right about Piper. She's holding her own with this case. She's been working on casting spells, strengthening her healing ability, and practicing her self-defense. Heck, she could turn out to be better at this hunting stuff than me."

My sweet Piper is something quite special, isn't she?

I'd already told Orwin that I wanted Piper to have the protection ward he'd put on himself months ago. It meant attempting to gather the same material components that were not easily accessible the first time around, but it would put my mind at ease that Ammeline couldn't do to Piper what she'd done to me and Knox.

I heard the two of you talking privately last week about this particular matter, and I've been meaning to express my appreciation for the concern you shower upon my sweet Piper.

"I'm the main reason Piper is about to confront a pack of werewolves, so let's just call it even. So, Jasper really went into the funeral home after leaving the diner?" I asked, averting the subject for our case. It was best to concentrate on solving this mystery so that we could head out of town and get our show on the road. "I don't get it, Pearl. I heard one of the diners say that the service doesn't begin until one o'clock. What did he do once he got inside?"

Mr. Jasper took a seat in the back of the room. I must admit that the flower arrangements around the wooden urn were absolutely beautiful. I have no doubt that Mr. Tommy Sutter's service will be quite elegant and give those remaining in this realm the closure they no doubt seek.

"Jasper must have gone into the funeral home for a reason," I surmised with respect. Pearl had easily discovered his presence in the diner, which meant he had done the same with her. He'd undeniably made the connection between the familiar and her witch. "Jasper went to the one place we couldn't go without drawing attention to ourselves, delaying our ability to find the answers we need."

You'll be pleased to know I was able to listen in to a

very nice gentleman who'd taken a phone call regarding a wake of sorts. Apparently, there is a small gathering planned at the town hall right after the service this afternoon.

"Our presence there would not only be disrespectful to the family, but it would also put us directly in the spotlight we've been trying to avoid. What we need to do is speak with Jasper, and he can't stay in the funeral home the entire day. So…"

Fine, dear hexed one. I can see where you're going with this conversation, and I agree that me keeping tabs on the local werewolf is the best course of action. With that said, I will be checking in with you periodically should any new information come to light.

I'd left the engine running so I could enjoy the heat coming out of the vents, and Pearl was gone by the time I'd turned off the engine. The last case Orwin and I had worked alone had taken close to a week to solve. With Piper and Pearl on board, we could theoretically cut that time in half. Add Knox into the equation, and we could actually be pulling out by sometime this evening.

"That would depend on when Knox returns," Orwin answered me right when I opened the door. I'd seen him come out of the RV, so I wasn't surprised he'd caught my last thought. "I haven't heard hide nor hair from him—no pun intended—but I did find out that Clyde's father at one point worked for Brady Buchanan. That was close to fifteen years ago, but you did say that we were looking for any type of connection."

"And Mason?" I asked, slamming the Jeep door and

pocketing my keys. I didn't like that Knox hadn't been able to return quickly, but I had no idea how far he had to travel to locate the pack. It was a moot point now, but I should have gotten his cell phone number. He'd taken his backpack, which meant he planned on walking at least partway in human form. "Did Mason or any of his family have any connection with the Buchanans?"

"Other than living in the same town, there was nothing that I could dig up. There used to be a summer camp back in the day, and the three victims did attend one of them around the age of ten. Unfortunately, so did the rest of the kids in town. I don't know if that helps with the case or not." Orwin glanced at his watch, clearly concerned about Knox as well. "Piper filled me in on what happened in town. She's inside on her laptop muttering something about discrepancies. Please tell me that you brought me breakfast. You left me here to starve."

I almost tried to punk him, but then I realized it would be useless. He could read my thoughts as easily as if I'd said the words aloud, so I reached into the Jeep and gave him the Denver omelet. Lunch was going to roll around soon enough, and I had a new plan in place.

"You're a wonderful person."

"I wish. No breakfast burritos, only traditional fare," I replied, laying my hand on his arm. There were times I got so caught up in a case or my hex that I sometimes came across as a less than attentive person, but I was trying to change. I was going to have to continue to work on that, because I wouldn't even be this far in my quest if it wasn't for Orwin. "I should have gotten you something else—"

"Apology accepted." Orwin pushed up his glasses with a smirk after he'd heard my true feelings on the subject. "And you're right. You wouldn't have gotten this far without me, and I know you're grateful. So grateful, in fact, you aren't going to be mad to find out that I ordered myself an NAS server."

I couldn't help but smile at the way Orwin had or-chestrated that entire discussion. We needed to be counting our pennies now that I'd invested so much into the RV, but he needed the right gear to make the job of researching our cases easier.

"You and I are going to take a ride back into town so you can ask the local mechanic about the tire we were having trouble with before we take a walk around town." I patted Orwin on the arm as I walked past him. "You're our best weapon right now to get the information we need."

"Can you please repeat that when Pearl is around? She won't believe me if I tell her you said that without collaboration."

It didn't take me long to tell Piper the new plan, with an added reassurance from her that she wouldn't leave the inside of the RV. She promptly reminded me of the arsenal of potions at her disposal, as well as multiple firearms of various types and calibers. I was walking back toward the Jeep when I spotted another vehicle. Orwin was leaning down and talking with Park Ranger Hank through the driver's side window.

"We'll meet you down at the station," Orwin called out with a tap on the hood of the car. "Thanks for letting us know."

Orwin began to walk toward me, but faltered in his step when he sneezed three times in succession. I followed his lead afterward, though, and walked over to the Jeep as the park ranger slowly inched forward until he passed us with a wave. Orwin had already pulled out a tissue.

"What was that about?" I asked cautiously, turning so I could monitor Park Ranger Hank's departure. I didn't have to be a witch to know that Orwin had picked up on something that would have this case becoming even more complex. Was that even possible? "Why would we go down to the police station?"

I didn't even know the town had a sheriff, which made this request even stranger. Orwin came away with a red nose by the time he'd finished using his tissue, and I realized that complex didn't even come close in describing what had taken place.

"You said you had some money left over after buying the RV, right?" Orwin asked in a nasally tone, his expression one of doubt. "Well, we're going to need some of it. It appears our new recruit got himself arrested for breaking and entering. Knox is currently sitting behind bars in the local jail."

Chapter Eleven

"I'D LIKE TO speak with Mr. Emeric in the meantime," I replied after it was explained that the sheriff was still over at the funeral home with no estimated time of when he'd return. According to the young officer manning the front desk of the police station, if you could even call it that. He stubbornly informed us that only the sheriff could authorize visitors. It didn't help my mood that we'd been given the runaround for an hour already, and I suspected it was for a very specific reason. My patience had reached the breaking point. "Has Mr. Emeric even been given his phone call or has the sheriff decided he won't be afforded that right, either?"

Orwin had quickly given me a read on the situation, although his allergies appeared to have gotten worse. Tyler was the young man's name. He hadn't even questioned me about how I'd known such a fact, even though there was no nameplate on his uniform. His only job had been to stall us, which he'd surprisingly been somewhat effective in his duties by feigning ignorance of the particulars in this case.

His success ended now.

"Deputy Tyler, I'm well aware Sheriff Jacobs asked you to stand guard and make sure we didn't have access to Mr. Emeric." Like I'd mentioned, my patience had worn thin. As a matter of fact, it had snapped in half. I'd decided to take a risk and hope it didn't backfire. Placing both hands on the counter separating the so-called waiting room from the rest of the office, I leaned forward and lowered my voice. "We're also aware that you've been wondering for some time how Sheriff Jacobs is getting away with some of the decisions he's made over the last five years, and this latest so-called arrest has you even more puzzled as to his motives. You're probably wondering how I know that, aren't you? Well, we know a lot about this town that would probably have you packing your bags in the next thirty seconds if you saw it in small print. Bottom line? You and I are both aware that Mr. Emeric wasn't breaking and entering into that cabin up north. He was investigating a lead. So, I'd suggest you let us speak with our colleague, unless of course you want a taskforce of federal agents to descend upon this peculiar tiny town that has somehow escaped scrutiny from the outside world."

Orwin had discovered that the sheriff had been the one to ensure certain details of the animal attacks hadn't made national news, with the help of the park ranger's office. Considering that Orwin could barely breath at the moment, it was a surefire bet that the sheriff belonged to the same pack as Jasper. Now, the two of them remained out of reach and holed up in the funeral home. There was always a chance I was wrong, and Orwin's worsening allergies were due to Knox being somewhere in the building, but that was highly unlikely.

"The feds?" Tyler appeared ready to swallow his tongue, so I'd definitely gotten my point across. "Let me call the sheriff over here. I don't think we need to take things that far."

"You sure got your point across to him," Orwin muttered as we both stood near the counter watching as Tyler walked toward the back of the small area and dug his cell phone out from the front pocket of his jeans. "His last thought I could pick up before he slipped out of range was that you *are* an undercover federal agent. He's calling the sheriff now to find out what he should do now that you basically threatened them with a full-blown FBI investigation, but now he's over six feet away from me. Do you read lips?"

I shot Orwin a wry glance before tapping my fingers on the counter. All that nervous tic did was remind me of Noah Martin. He'd somehow guessed what had killed Tommy, but did he suspect anyone in town of being the culprit?

"You're assuming that's why Noah was out at the campsite last night. He could have been simply trying to give his girlfriend some closure." Orwin sneezed, which he had been doing pretty much ever since we'd entered this town. His allergies today seemed particularly worse, which led me to believe I was right about the sheriff being of the same species as Jasper. "I know it probably seems disrespectful to go to the funeral home, but I could always go over and ask to speak to the sheriff about official business."

"Pearl's been saying that I don't look at the silver lining often enough," I tossed out, contemplating that now might a good time to take her advice. I noticed that Tyler seemed to be whispering into his phone as he regarded us cautiously, telling me that the sheriff was most likely trying to get his minion to stall us a bit longer. "Knox being behind bars gives us valid reason to stay in town until this is resolved."

"That's cold, Lou." Orwin still seemed to consider my theory while leaning an elbow on the counter. "Come to think of it, he does owe us. I mean, he followed us around for over three months. He studied our movements, listened in on our conversations, and basically did recon on our activities to gather intel that he would have used himself had this particular case regarding his own kind not come up on his radar."

I couldn't help but arch an eyebrow at the way Orwin had rationalized leaving Knox behind bars a little longer than necessary.

"And you say I'm cold?"

"What? You can't stand there and tell me that what

you think Emeric did was right," Orwin stated with exaggerated incredulity. He walked back over to the three chairs lined up against the display window and took a seat, getting tired of standing while we waited for Tyler to finish his phone call with the sheriff. "It's one thing for Pearl to make light of my conspiracy theories, but it's another for a virtual stranger to listen in on me giving statistics on UFO sightings. He doesn't know me, and he might think that—"

"That you're off your meds?" I offered up with a smile. Orwin's conspiracy quirk was one of the reasons I liked having him around. It also meant that he was willing to think outside the box. And in our current line of business, that was a good thing. "It's okay. If any human were to hear Knox's story, they'd most likely commit him to a mental institution and throw away the key."

Movement outside caught my eye. I shifted my focus over Orwin's right shoulder, somewhat taken aback to find that Noah was in the midst of having an argument with a very pretty brunette as they crossed the street. Trust me, it was easy to tell that she wasn't happy from the grimace draped across her face and the way she was moving her hands in an obvious sign of agitation.

"Orwin, you need to—"

"Excuse me," Tyler said, interrupting my request to have Orwin go outside and get close enough to Noah in order to get a read on his thoughts. "The sheriff is asking that you wait right here while he finishes up some business. He said that he shouldn't be too much longer, and then he'll handle your issue."

Handle my issue? It sounded as though we were finally going to be able to speak with Knox and find out exactly what happened up near that cabin. Was there something or someone inside that could help solve this case? I guess I'd find out soon enough. In the meantime, Orwin didn't have to remain inside the police station when he could gather information by simply stepping outside.

"We'll see about that, Tyler. I appreciate your—"

"Lou, it's a stall tactic," Orwin exclaimed, practically falling out of the chair to get to his feet. He sneezed two times before he could explain more in depth, all the while Tyler taking two steps back from the counter with a look of horror. "They took Knox out the back door. Go!"

"How did you know—"

We both made a run for the front door, ignoring Tyler's stunned realization that he'd failed to distract us. Orwin barged through first, not even glancing at the arguing couple. He ran down the sidewalk and made a quick left around the building. He pressed his right hand against the brick to give him better traction. I was close on his heels, just in time to hear an engine pull away.

Having Knox transported somewhere else could have massive repercussions, especially given his ability to change into a werewolf at will. Would he do so in order to escape, thereby threatening to expose the supernatural secret we all shared?

I instinctively raised my hand, knowing full well I could chuck a dumpster in the path of the vacating vehicle. Orwin quickly knocked my hand to the side before I expanded the energy I'd collected from the earth below, even stepping in front of me to prevent my attempt at fixing a relatively complicated situation.

"There's no difference between Knox turning and you casting magic," Orwin muttered, his gaze focusing on something...most likely, someone...over my shoulder. "Well, besides the full-blown panic of seeing a man transform into a beast. Either way, you're chancing someone finding out what we really are."

"Tell me that wasn't Knox," I pleased, a little bit out of breath. I was in relatively good shape, especially getting in all the self-defense moves I'd been teaching Piper recently. It had more to do with the cold air hitting my lungs after having been cooped up inside their little police station. "A dumpster could have moved for any rational reason. I could have made sure he remained here in town, and now we've missed our chance. We have no idea where the sheriff is taking Knox. This is bad, Orwin. Real bad."

A quick glance over my shoulder revealed that Lisa Sutter and Noah Martin had followed us after they'd seen we were running toward something. They were a good thirty feet away, so Orwin wouldn't be able to pick up any thoughts that could aid in our investigation.

"No, it's not. You should know that I always have an ace up my sleeve. First, it wasn't the sheriff who was driving," Orwin said, instantly gaining my full attention. He eyed the back door that no doubt led to the detention area and the specific jail cell Knox had been held in all morning. "Sheriff Jacobs must still be at the funeral home. Second, there were people watching us too closely for you to use magic. Not to fret, because as an added bonus, I already know where Knox is being taken."

My anger spiked at being duped by Tyler. Some of these residents were giving us the runaround, which lent me to believe that some of them knew more than they were saying. Take Jasper, who was still at the funeral home. He held the answers we were seeking, he could potentially save lives, but etiquette was preventing us from crashing the funeral.

Speaking of funerals.

I turned around to find that Noah and Lisa had already vanished, most likely to attend her brother's service.

"Etiquette is Pearl's specialty, so you'll have to see if there's a way around crashing a funeral." Orwin walked over to the back door of the police station, but it was locked. We'd have to go around to the front. Maybe by the time I reached the counter, I'd be a bit more composed. At the rate at which I was clenching my fist, I

might just end up sending Tyler through the back wall.
"No violence permitted."

Did someone mention violence?

"Pearl, we have a problem." For once, the feline's
interruption hadn't given me a start. All three of us
started back around the building, although only two of
us could be visually seen. "Knox was arrested, the sheriff
is sending him…"

"To the county jail," Orwin chimed in when I
paused in my update.

"And we still haven't found out anything new. I
know it's disrespectful, but I need to crash that funeral,
Pearl."

*Oh, my! I have missed quite a lot while I've been other-
wise occupied with the local werewolf. First things first—we
do not need to resort to such blatant insolence, dear hexed
one. Not on my watch.*

"Then you're going to need to find a way to smoke
out Jasper or Sheriff Jacobs for a conversation." We'd
made it back to the front of the building and were
standing near the glass door of the police station. To any
onlookers, it appeared that Orwin and I were having a
discussion with one another. "We're wasting precious
time that we could be using to seek out that medium
regarding Ammeline. Jasper escaped into that funeral
home just so that he wouldn't be forced to talk with us,
and he's going to find out that we aren't going to take no
for an answer."

I will do your bidding, Miss Lilura, but only because

I've discovered something that might interest you while observing Mr. Jasper. You see, the lingering aroma of wet dog in the air does not only belong to the convenience store attendant. The moment the sheriff made an entrance, I realized then that he had something in common with Jasper.

"Sheriff Jacobs is a werewolf. Unfortunately, we found out that hard way. Orwin might end up getting a sinus infection by the time this case is over." It was a good thing that Knox had been given a ward in regard to his body scent, so the sheriff wouldn't have known about Knox's abilities. The same wasn't true for Knox, and he'd purposefully kept his secret hidden from the sheriff. Why? "We need to find out what Knox found up near that isolated cabin."

You certainly know how to hamper a good discovery, dear hexed one. Fortunately learning that Sheriff Jacobs is a werewolf isn't the only thing I've found during my rounds. Upon listening in on a conversation between the sheriff and Mr. Nelson, I found it very odd that the request of ashes had been made. I'm not quite sure what to make of such a demand, though it sounds quite sacrilegious, if you ask me.

"Ashes?" I'd become rather lost in this fact-finding mission. "What do you mean, someone made a request for ashes?"

Sheriff Jacobs inquired to Nelson about obtaining more ashes, though someone interrupted their discussion. I will attempt to find out more, but may we please get back to Mr. Emeric? How do you propose we go about getting him back into the fold?

"I know this is going to sound odd," Orwin began, and the smile on his face told me he'd come up with a doozy of a plan, "but does Piper know how to hotwire a vehicle?"

Oh, dear.

Chapter Twelve

"WHAT DO YOU mean, they're gone?"

Mr. Jasper and Sheriff Jacobs are no longer in the funeral home, Miss Lilura. I've explained this twice already. I can only assume they realized I'd vacated the building for a few moments and took advantage of my absence to abscond.

We'd finally implemented a strategy on how to obtain the answers we sought, and nothing—I mean, nothing—was going according to the new plan. Piper had used a spell to hotwire Knox's Land Rover after Orwin explaining the wires for ten minutes had gotten us nowhere. She was currently on her way to intercept the vehicle taking Knox to the county jail.

You have no worries about my sweet Piper. She has the sleeping potion that she'll use on the driver, and he'll have no memory of what transpired during Mr. Emeric's dramatic escape.

"It's not Piper I'm worried about," I murmured, watching the front entrance of the funeral home from inside the warm Jeep. The mourners were beginning to arrive and making their way inside. "Where would the sheriff and Jasper have gone?"

I checked the gas station. An older woman was sitting on a stool behind the cash register. As far as I could tell, she was not a werewolf. Maybe we should start a list to keep everyone straight.

Orwin was grabbing us a couple of sandwiches from the diner. We had no idea if Piper would need help with Knox's escape, so I wanted to be ready to go should she send an emergency text. Of course, Pearl would be able to reach her first, but I wasn't comfortable leaving Piper alone to accomplish such a risky endeavor.

My sweet Piper has things under control. I just checked in with her, and she's pulled the Land Rover onto the side of the road far enough away from town that no one should witness her heroic act. Her hazard lights are flashing, and she's ready to flag down the police vehicle in which Mr. Emeric is ensconced in the backseat.

"Pearl, would you please go into the funeral home and listen in on the conversations? Someone has to know where Jasper and the sheriff have gone," I said, an uncomfortable sensation rolling up my spine. It wasn't due to Pearl cracking a joke about two werewolves being in a funeral home, either. "At least, one should think it was odd for Jasper to have been inside for hours, only to disappear at the same time as the sheriff. Right?"

There was no answer, and I had no idea how long Pearl had been gone. Talk about lacking in the etiquette department. I'd definitely have to bring this moment up sometime in the near future.

"That's being spiteful," Orwin pointed out, having opened the passenger side door. The delicious aroma of sweet chili filled the Jeep, and my stomach rumbled. It was the perfect meal on such a cold and dreary day. "I knew you'd want chili over a sandwich. Score one for the thoughtful warlock. Did you know that Janet thinks aliens are the cause of the strange things that go on in this town?"

"Who's Jan...oh. The waitress. Really?" I took the lid off the Styrofoam bowl, inhaling the delectable scent. Orwin held up a spoon after he'd set two to-go cups in the console. Mine would no doubt have ice water inside. "I'm beginning to think the entire town is in on this caper. Why aliens?"

I maintained my focus on the front entrance of the funeral home as I devoured my lunch, not having really eaten since last night when we were on the road. I'd heated up a microwave dinner that tasted more like plastic than food. Nourishment was needed for hunts like these, and I was close to making a decision that would put us right in the thick of things.

"Janet was telegraphing her thoughts like a beacon, so it was hard to miss," Orwin shared after swallowing down a bite of his sandwich. He actually seemed a bit uplifted that someone else was sure aliens had visited our planet. "She saw a beam of light come from the woods behind her house years ago. Her husband was out at the bar that night, so she took her dog and a flashlight to go see if someone had gotten lost. For some reason, she was thinking about the memory while she was ringing up our lunch order. She saw the silhouette of something standing on two legs, at least seven feet tall."

"A werewolf," I fathomed, pretty confident in my deduction given our circumstances. I stopped eating while I gave that some thought. "How many years ago?"

"It's not like Janet thought the number in her head as she was thinking about the alien, Lou." Orwin took a sip of his drink after shaking his head at my question. "The only reason I know the incident took place years ago was because she was also thinking about cutting her hair to the same style back then. She's worried she'll regret it and that it will take years to grow it out to where she has it now."

"Wow," I exclaimed, dipping the spoon in my chili so that I could take a drink of my water. "I don't know how you handle all that information overload. I'd lose my—"

Speaking of information overload, I've come back with quite the motherlode of golden information.

Orwin's sandwich landed in his lap at Pearl's unexpected interruption. Technically, her appearance wasn't unforeseen, but she did have a knack of inducing adrenaline rushes. On the bright side, which I was trying to look at more and more after being lectured about my pessimistic outlook by Pearl, he'd set the Styrofoam container on his lap to catch any droppings.

"Welcome to my world," I muttered before readjusting my rearview mirror. Sure enough, Pearl was sitting as prim and proper as could be in the middle of the back seat. It was finally time to get down to business. "Please tell me that your motherlode of information will lead us to the werewolf and his pal responsible for the attacks."

For starters, Sheriff Jacobs told Mr. Brady that he was going to get an update from the park rangers. Mr. Brady was reassuring Mr. Sutter that they would have answers soon or else they'll try once again to take matters into their own hands.

"That makes no sense," I said, trying to put the pieces together. I wasn't having any luck. "The sheriff knows exactly what is going on in his town. He's buying himself time, but for what?"

"Let's not forget about Jasper." Orwin closed the Styrofoam lid on his container and wiped his fingers on a napkin. He scratched his nose. Being in this town was havoc on his health. "He had to have snuck out the back the same time as the sheriff. If they left together, it sure wasn't to go talk to the park rangers."

"The sheriff's involvement certainly explains the lack of national interest in these so-called animal attacks. He's managed to keep the real story a secret." I took Orwin's cue and sealed the plastic lid over what was left of my chili. He held the plastic bag open so that I could toss my things into it before making a decision that would end up taking us farther away from Piper should she need assistance. I wasn't sure that was the right choice, though. "He has the ability to report these murders any way he sees fit, thereby squashing national interest."

Moving on to the next tidbit of information, I witnessed the funeral director deflect Mrs. Sutter's questions about the state of her son. Now, I usually respect anyone who displays proper manners, but Mr. Nelson was acting rather peculiar. A little too much, if you ask me, especially after being asked about securing more ashes for the sheriff.

Orwin took one of the unused napkins and promptly sneezed.

"Well, remember when we were at the diner earlier?" I wasn't willing to write off Pearl's assessment, but it could be explained. "It was said by the two couples at the table to the right of us that Benji or Brady didn't want Mrs. Sutter to be left with such a horrible vision of her son. Maybe Nelson was protecting them during their time of grief. As for the ashes, I'm not quite sure why the sheriff would request such a thing."

I do recall that conversation. I'll come back to that then, once I've had time to analyze Mr. Nelson's peculiar behavior. In the meantime, we must head back to the campsite immediately.

"Why would we return to the campsite?" Orwin asked, looking a bit peeved that his allergies had come back full force. "What we need to do is find Sheriff Jacobs and Jasper. They're the werewolves, so they have to know who's responsible for the murders."

I beg to differ. We need to—

"That's it," I realized, leaning forward and starting

the engine to the Jeep. Excitement coursed through my veins that this case could finally be closed. "Sheriff Jacobs and Jasper know the guilty party. The sheriff arrested Knox near that isolated cabin up on the mountainside, which could mean that is where they are holding the werewolves responsible."

The two of you are not listening. I'm not done—

"The sheriff didn't want Knox to stumble over their rogue werewolves, having no idea that Knox is one himself or more than capable of protecting himself," Orwin continued to verbally route where my thoughts had taken me. He tossed the used napkin in with the rest of the garbage before tying a knot in the plastic. "Lou, if the rogue werewolves are members of this pack, you realize that it's best they handle its disposition."

A quick glance at my side mirror told me that no one was driving past, so I slowly pulled the Jeep onto the road and headed the opposite direction of the campsite. I'd studied the map enough to know that there was an access road to the mountain about a mile from here. We could be at the cabin in about thirty minutes, barring there were no downed trees or roadblocks.

"I would agree with you, with the exception of the second wolf. How can we be sure that the sheriff or Jasper even knows about—"

Manners, my valued colleagues! Where are your manners? One does not interrupt someone when they are not finished with their story. Now, as I was saying…

Orwin and I shared an apologetic look, not having meant to offend Pearl. We'd worked alone together for quite a while, and it took some time getting used to having others around to consider.

Consider? I'm what you say is your ace in the hole, dear hexed one. And you're headed in the wrong direction. We must first locate one Noah Martin.

"Noah?" I didn't bother to flip on my turn signal, because I was determined to see exactly who the sheriff was keeping up at the cabin. There was a good chance that the sheriff or Jasper would be moving their prisoners now that Knox had key information, which meant we couldn't wait for Piper to spring Knox from the back of a police car. "Noah was inside the funeral home."

Was *being the operative word, Miss Lilura. Mr. Noah was not in the funeral home, which suggests that he's heading back to the campsite to finish what he started last night. I can think of no other reason he would leave Ms. Sutter's side.*

I remained silent, knowing full well that both Pearl and Orwin could read my thoughts. One of the advantages of having *valued colleagues* as Pearl had mentioned time again was that we had the ability to split our resources. Noah could have run back to the house for some reason or maybe gone to the town hall to make sure things were set up for the gathering afterward. We couldn't afford to waste over forty minutes driving to and from the opposite direction. Besides, Noah wouldn't be in danger if the real threat was still up at that cabin.

And pray tell, dear hexed one, what would you like a defenseless kitty such as myself to do once I reach the campsite alone?

The sound that came from Orwin definitely wasn't a sneeze.

I wasn't going for humor that time, Mr. Cornelia. I was merely pointing out that is how Mr. Martin might view me. Back to my inquiry, dear hexed one.

"I'm sure you'll figure something out," I said, having no doubt that Pearl was resourceful. We were coming upon one of the access roads that would lead us up the mountain. Orwin had cracked his window, most likely hoping to get some fresh air to relieve a bit of his allergies. "Once Piper secures Knox, they'll be closer to you should you need help. If Noah isn't up at the campsite, come straight to the cabin. I'll give Piper a call and tell her about the plan we have in place."

I'd like to stipulate that I'm not very fond of this plan. Not at all.

"Sheriff Jacobs and Jasper have to know of that second wolf." I checked my rearview mirror, making sure that no one was behind us. The coast was clear, and I made the turn that would lead us to our destination. "It's also safer to disclose our true identities up at the cabin. Once we ensure there are no humans in the area, we can then have ourselves a heart to heart with the sheriff and Jasper about their rogue werewolf and whoever could be the second threat to their town."

I won't be but a jiffy. There are too many variables in

play. In my experience, that is usually when the "you know what" hits the fan. Please, don't do anything that jeopardizes your lives. After all, Mr. Cornelia has the keys to the RV. That would prove rather inconvenient. In case you haven't made the connection between dogs and cats, my being stuck in werewolf territory is not so good for my health.

Chapter Thirteen

THE AREA WHERE Knox had been arrested finally came into view through the trees. At least, this was the place if Tyler had told the truth. Orwin and I remained in the Jeep while we carefully took in our surroundings. Sure enough, Sheriff Jacobs' official police vehicle was parked at an odd angle out front of the cabin. His patrol car was the only sign of life within seeing distance.

Orwin and I remained quiet, figuring those inside had already heard our approach from a mile away. That was the trouble when dealing with werewolves—their extraordinary senses were like no others. If they were going to ambush us, it would be in werewolf form out here in the forest.

Bottom line was that there no use in giving them more ammunition by hearing us discuss a plan. Orwin shot me a look that basically asked me what plan I was even talking about, but I hadn't gotten that far. Had we been able to reach Piper, I wouldn't have been so paranoid.

Had something gone wrong with the rescue? How hard could it be to liberate a werewolf?

Orwin shook his head at my mental inquiry, looking down at his phone and pushing his glasses up the bridge of his nose. He quickly sent another text. We sure didn't want to initiate a call so close to prying ears, and we certainly didn't want the sheriff to know that we'd hopefully retrieved our colleague. I'm sure an alert would be sent out the moment the officer or whoever had been driving the vehicle awoke to being handcuffed to his steering wheel.

I lifted my gaze back up to the cabin, wondering if Jasper had joined the sheriff in driving up here. Once again, I noted no movement. Were they inside the cabin trying to decide the fate of one of their own? There was no room for disloyalty among the pack, and there were harsh punishments doled out for the murder of an innocent in packs that didn't feed on humans.

Honestly, I had no desire to get involved with pack business. All I wanted was to share vital information that would help them figure out who the guilty party's accomplice was to cause such destruction upon the town and spread fear amongst its residents.

I scanned the edge of the woods to my right. Not even a single brown leaf moved on the ground in the light breeze. It was as if the wildlife sensed predators in their midst, leaving them with only one choice—running for their lives.

Both Orwin and I startled when his phone rang and broke the ominous silence.

"Great," I muttered, wincing at the loud sound. "Nothing like making a grand entrance."

If the werewolves had been busy amongst themselves and strangely happened to have missed our arrival, they certainly knew we were here now. I reached for the handle of the door, figuring it was best to be out in the open where I could defend myself. Being cooped up in the Jeep wouldn't give me a lot of room to utilize the energy of the earth under my feet to my benefit.

Orwin had already answered the call, but it was clear after the third time he'd said Piper's name that the signal this high up was extremely bad. It was probably for the best, considering that the front door of the cabin had slowly opened to reveal Jasper in human form.

It was good to know that I'd gotten something right over the course of this case. Now, negotiations could begin.

"Jasper, I know you're aware that I'm a witch," I began, not even bothering to raise my voice. He could hear me just fine. I made my way around to the front of the Jeep, hearing Orwin exit his side of the vehicle. I'd left my door open just in case I needed to make a quick dash toward a getaway, though that would be after whatever battle might occur. I wasn't foolish enough to believe I could get away unscathed, especially when there was a whole pack involved. "It's why you went inside the funeral home, counting on the fact that I wouldn't want to cause a scene or more stress to the Sutter family."

"Leave," Jasper ordered, raising his raspy voice so that I wouldn't have trouble understanding his directive. "You don't belong here."

As if to confirm Jasper's declaration, Orwin sneezed three times in succession.

"I completely understand that this is pack business, but I'm not sure you're aware that you're not dealing with just one rogue wolf." I began to close the distance between us, every one of my senses heightened by the exposure I was placing myself in. Orwin came to stand next to me. I didn't have to look down at his waist to know that his special silver bladed dagger was at the ready. I was determined there would be no bloodshed, though. "I just want to speak to whoever the Alpha is in order for him to know what brought us here."

Jasper wasn't the Alpha.

That much was obvious.

No one in charge of the pack would have exposed himself by walking out of that cabin into the presence of a witch and warlock.

"I won't say it again—leave. You have no business here."

Does no one have manners in this town? Good heavens, these creatures need a class in etiquette.

"Now isn't the time, Pearl," Orwin muttered, barely moving his mouth. No doubt Jasper had gotten a whiff of the sleek familiar the moment she'd materialized. Don't get me wrong. She remained invisible, but her scent most likely permeated the air. "Did you take care of that other problem?"

Unfortunately, that's what I've come to report. Mr. Martin was nowhere to be found, and he certainly did not drive to the campsite. His vehicle is still at the funeral home, but it seems as if he's simply vanished. As long as we see to this matter you currently seem to be having trouble with, we can do the same for the other. These mangy creatures can take care of their own rogue beast, and this town can return to its version of normal as it has done so in the past. Besides, Mr. Cornelia is looking a bit worse for wear.

"Jasper, we can continue standing here with two separate objectives in mind until nightfall. We're not leaving until I've met with your Alpha and he's heard what I've come to say. Would you please—"

Jasper might have been an older gentleman, but that didn't prevent him from displaying his strength. His cloudy blue eyes suddenly became dark before practically glowing in anger at my insistence to speak to his Alpha.

My, Mr. Jasper certainly displays an unwelcoming attitude, does he not? Considering my age, he cannot use that as an excuse.

One second Jasper was on the porch and the next he was thirty feet in front of us. Orwin immediately palmed his silver bladed knife, and I instinctively raised my hand with every intention of tossing him back the way he'd come.

Jasper had not made the complete change, but his eyes continued to glow as he growled, proudly showing his elongated teeth. The only problem I could foresee for Orwin and me was that we didn't know if the entire pack was in attendance. Being outnumbered would definitely turn the tide of the battle against us.

I realize that now is not the time to bring this up into the conversation, but I did strongly advise against this little side trip. Mr. Cornelia, are you crying or are your eyes just watering from the dander hanging in the air?

"You don't want to do this, Jasper. You're at a disadvantage here." How much more direct could I be? I'd already asserted we weren't a threat, and that all I wanted to do was share information that could help their pack. We couldn't leave this town without making sure that both perpetrators were dealt with accordingly.

I think it's time I check in with Piper while you sort out this snafu with Grandpa Werewolf. I'll see how far away they are, just in case you need the additional help. I'll also see if they can bring Mr. Cornelia's allergy medicine.

"Jasper." The deep, rich voice didn't come from the sheriff. In fact, I was a bit surprised to see Matt step out from the line of trees to our left. I hadn't seen him since last night at the gas station, and I honestly hadn't given him a thought since then. He'd been the one who'd warned us about the animal attacks, which now gave me pause. "I'll take care of this…issue. Go back inside."

Something wasn't right, and I was at a loss in figuring out what we'd missed. Having Knox here would definitely have aided in sorting through the testosterone hanging in the air. As if to confirm my thought, Orwin sneezed again. My only hope was that he didn't turn blue. It wasn't like I could call a time out in this situation.

"Miss Lilura. You didn't heed my advice about getting as far from this town as possible. I'm suggesting you turn around and do so now."

I had a feeling I'd just met the Alpha of this territory.

"That would be a correct assumption, given the number of glowing eyes peering out from the forest," Orwin muttered in misery. He sniffled in agitation. "You should know I've made a decision. I'm sitting out the next werewolf case. This exposure isn't good for my health."

"Let's hope there is a next," I replied cautiously, scanning the tree line behind Matt and attempting to count the other hairy beasts who had completely transformed. Maybe five? "I tend to make my own decisions, Matt. You want to tell me why you allowed one of your betas to encourage us to stay at the campsite when you clearly wanted us out of the area?"

"I'm sorry about that." Matt didn't appear sorry in the least. It was clear in the way he carried himself that he was the Alpha. I can't believe I hadn't seen it before, but he'd camouflaged his authoritative air behind a uniform. Any outsider wouldn't have seen the difference, which was why he'd gone for such a position. I'd certainly fell for it. He wasn't wearing his utility belt, but why would he do so up in the mountains when he could easily turn into a predator within seconds? "Jasper's been around for quite a while. He's the kind who always takes a yard when you give him that first inch."

Speaking of Jasper, he hadn't gone back inside the cabin. He really did have trouble taking orders.

"Reminds me of Pearl," Orwin said in an effort to remain calm. He got this way from time to time. I called it his chatty phase, which signaled he thought we might be in big trouble. "In case you haven't noticed, we're outnumbered. By a lot. And that's not counting those werewolves in the cabin."

"Let's cut to the chase then, Matt." I didn't like being at a disadvantage, and that's exactly what Orwin had purposefully pointed out. Unfortunately, I wasn't sure there was a way out of this situation that didn't involve some type of hand to hand combat. "Three murders occurred within an eight-week timespan at two campsites in close proximity. You've ordered Sheriff Jacobs to cover for one of your own, which is why the animal attacks aren't being reported as national news. What you don't realize is that another member of your pack is also involved."

"I'm well aware of what happens in my territory, Miss Lilura. Now, you and your friend best be on your way."

Matt continued to stand on the edge of the tree line

without a jacket, staring back at me with an intensity that was all but a warning of what would occur should I dismiss his suggestion. I quickly ran through the timeline, recognizing the glitch we'd somehow missed.

Ashes.

Was it possible?

Had there been no murders at all?

"Oh, that's low," Orwin replied with disgust. "That's lower than low."

"Answer me one thing before I go, Matt," I called out, appreciating that Orwin had shifted with me and was covering my six in case a member of the pack decided to attack from the opposite direction. "Given your body language, it's apparent the offenders you're dealing with are in that cabin. But they weren't rogue attacks, were they? Mason, Clyde, and Tommy were all initiated. You faked their deaths, and then you had help covering the initiation by the sheriff and Nelson. Am I pretty close to the truth?"

I could literally feel the tension coming off of Orwin as he'd connected the dots, too. We were most likely going to end up in an all-out war with a pack of werewolves. If Matt claimed that he'd been holding three individuals for days, then last night's attempted attack on Noah Martin had been planned by the Alpha himself.

We had saved a life during this case, but Noah Martin was now missing.

"Noah's probably inside," Orwin speculated, much

as I already had in regard to the sheriff and Jasper leaving the funeral home. It hadn't been because of Pearl, but to protect their own kind. It was now easy to figure out that Noah must have seen Tommy after his so-called death, somehow put things together, and the pack had no choice but to change him like the others. That's what I'd seen during my vision. "This situation just got a bit hairier."

"I've never been a big fan of puns," Matt replied with a frown. His arms had been crossed, but he slowly lowered them to his side. Orwin and I both tensed at the indication of attack. "As I said, you have no business being in my territory. This is your one and only chance to leave. Please don't force my hand and have this result in bloodshed for any of us."

I was getting really tired of being put in situations that resulted in either curses or bloodshed. Maybe Pearl had a point. Etiquette seemed to have gone out the window, but I can at least say that I tried to be nice. We were going to have no choice but to handle this with magic, and I was confident that Orwin was reading my thoughts on the strategy I'd come up with that would hopefully bring an end to the attacks.

"It's hard to concentrate after hearing the word *bloodshed*," Orwin muttered as he was most likely attempting to count the number of adversaries we were about to undertake. He used his shoulder to push up his glasses. "I love the confidence, Lou, but in case you haven't notice…we're a little outnumbered."

Orwin had the advantage in hand to hand combat

due to his ability with telepathy. He knew where, when, and how his adversary would attack due to the close proximity, thus giving him the ability to sidestep a lethal blow.

"You should listen to your companion, Miss Lilura," Matt called out rather smugly after hearing every single word Orwin and I had exchanged. "This is your last chance to walk away with your pride intact."

Pride?

Orwin might have groaned at Matt's provocation. It had garnered the opposite result that I'm sure the Alpha was hoping for, but he had no idea that I'd lost my pride close to four months ago with my unpredicted run in with the only Queen Lich in existence. My surge of anger most likely would have been the cause of an all-out war had Matt's eyes not glowed even more and swung toward the cabin.

It was clear that something was happening inside that was cause for concern.

"…won't allow a witch to mess this up!"

Matt took off at a run toward the cabin the moment a long howl pierced the air, but he was too late to stop the beast coming through the front door.

I was his target.

As fast and powerful as Matt might be, he wouldn't reach the werewolf before it reached me. I did the only thing I could in self-defense—I utilized the harnessed energy from the earth and lifted the police car off the ground, tossing it in the air to block the beast's most direct path.

Unfortunately, the thunderous crash it made upon landing back down onto the ground was not enough to deter the oversized creature. He'd lunged out of the way of the metal obstacle, landing on the side of the vehicle and all but crushing part of the door with its large clawed feet. His snout rose in the air and sniffed the scents around us, and his deep guttural growl and hesitance told me that help had finally arrived…and not a moment too soon.

Oh, dear. I can't leave the two of you alone for a second, can I? The situation seems to have gotten a bit out of hand since I've been gone, Miss Lilura.

"Stand down or suffer the consequences!" Matt declared, his throaty growl echoing through the enclosed open area. "Obey my authority or I will leave you to fend for yourself, Tommy."

The Alpha now stood between us and the threat, though his decision to place himself in such a precarious situation had caused the other werewolves to show themselves. I quickly counted nine—no, eleven— members of Matt's pack closing in around us.

It's good to know the two of you are caught up. Tommy Sutter is alive and well, standing on top of that mangled vehicle. That description, of course, might be a bit of a stretch considering he's turned into a filthy beast and apparently wants to maim you and Mr. Cornelia for your interference. I digress, though. Help should be arriving momentarily, dear hexed one.

Chapter Fourteen

"I DON'T KNOW about you, but I'm having a hard time wrapping my mind around this. Why would they disguise new members as deaths and risk outing themselves?" Orwin asked in confusion, not removing his gaze from the standoff before us. The air was thick with tension, and it was as if one misconstrued move would initiate a combat unlike any other we've ever seen. "Lou, now might be a good time to rethink that plan of yours."

Plan? I've already explained that reinforcements will be arriving shortly. You really should listen when someone is talking, alien hunter. A slight postponement is all that is needed.

I'll admit that finding out Tommy Sutter, Mason Leeds, and Clyde Simmons were alive had been rather eye-opening. Granted, they were now werewolves, but they were still alive.

I'd heard that part loud and clear, and that counted for something.

As a matter of fact, I replayed Tommy's words over and over in my mind about not wanting a witch to mess things up, but I was still struggling to understand the meaning behind them.

My sweet Piper said much the same thing when Mr. Emeric tried to explain what he'd discovered here. It is all very confusing, and it is certainly a mess that needs to be straightened out before we can be on our way. That is, if Tommy doesn't attempt to eat us first. Is he looking a bit feral or is it just the overcast lighting?

"Matt, rein in your new recruit," I called out loudly, my directive only serving to anger Tommy further. He even took a step forward, causing the vehicle to rock underneath him. It was then that I could see the cut on his thigh. He'd been injured when I'd attempted to block his advance, but I wasn't the only one trying to prevent a violent skirmish. Whatever was taking place here did not have Matt's full backing or else he would have allowed Tommy to attack us. "You've seen what I can do, and that's only a small fraction of my power. I came here believing that humans were being taken out by a rogue member of your faction. From where we're standing, it looks as if this situation has gotten out of hand, so I'm not leaving here without an explanation and a promise that no more deaths will occur in this town due to one of your members—and that includes Noah Martin."

You make us sound like the police force of the supernatural. I quite like it, dear hexed one.

Matt was facing Tommy, but he'd turned his head just so in order to cast me a warning glance. The gilded glow of his eyes glistened with rebuke. The fact that he was not willing to turn his back on a newly turned werewolf warned me that he didn't have complete control of the situation we'd found ourselves in. I had to wonder if Tommy was not making some sort of move to claim the title of Alpha.

"Uh, Lou." Orwin nudged me, but I'd already seen that the other wolves had completely surrounded us. "I'm not liking these odds. Pearl, what's the ETA on those reinforcements?"

Patience, alien hunter.

The palms of my hands began to perspire with uneasiness. I wasn't sure patience came into play here, especially seeing Sheriff Jacobs finally make an appearance. He wasn't alone, and I recognized the other two men by his side immediately.

They all slowly come around either end of the vehicle to join Jasper. Their focus was trained on Tommy, and none of them seemed too happy with the current circumstances. It was good to see that they were taking their Alpha's lead and standing guard should the unpredictable lycanthrope try and come after me. Unfortunately, it wasn't very comforting knowing that the werewolves responsible for this entire debacle were only now attempting to rein in an already precarious situation.

"Tommy, trust me when I say that you don't want to fight me," Matt warned, holding up a fist when the others went to close in. "I did you and your friends a solid. I kept my promise, took care of the loose ends, helped you navigate the change, and paved the way for you to take over a territory up north far away from my territory. But if you start a war with these witches on my turf…I will destroy you."

You know, alien hunter, I might actually go see what is keeping them. Try and keep the peace while I'm gone.

The transformation from wolf to human—well, semi-human—didn't seem as painful as the opposite. Within seconds, Tommy Sutter had become more of a version of himself, maintaining his glowing eyes of desperation. Piper had shown me his photograph during her research, and the half-man/half-wolf standing on top of the police vehicle was definitely Tommy Sutter.

"You'd protect this witch and her friends over your own kind?" Tommy yelled out in anger. It had only been a week since his transformation. His emotions were no doubt all over the map, and he certainly wasn't thinking clearly. He was a powder keg ready to explode. "I was raised in this town, Matt. Loyalty above all else, isn't that pack creed?"

The tension in the air was rising, but this standoff took the focus from Orwin and me. It was the smallest of opportunities that we needed to control the narrative. I'd been memorizing some of the incantations that were more instantaneous, but there had been one I'd come across that had been relatively easy to learn.

"*Sit natuura quaedam, ut impius inveniamus. Folia*

tradimus ligaveruntque eum omnis erit finis," I murmured, lowering my hands so that the energy of the earth could flow through me and do my bidding. I repeated the phrase, taking the time given to me to gain the upper hand. At this point, I had to use everything at my disposal. "*Sit natuura quaedam, ut impius inveniamus. Folia tradimus ligaveruntque eum omnis erit finis.*"

"Are you sure that's a good idea?" Orwin asked quietly, having already sensed the electrical component in the air. The spell I was casting wasn't immediate. The roots of the trees slowly slithered out from underneath the foliage, aiming for their targets. "The werewolves are already noticing something is wrong with their environment, and it's not like we don't already have an explosive situation in front of us."

I never hesitated in my mantra. Pearl had reassured us that Piper and Knox were close by, and we needed to trust that they would be here for us in our time of need.

I'm glad to see my words of wisdom have made an effect on you, dear hexed one. As for your incantation, it couldn't have come at a better time. It's camouflaging the fact that we're about to get a visitor...a rather large one at that. You'll finally understand the difference between a standard northwestern grey wolf and a Canis Lupus Occidentalis of the McKenzie Valley variant. Their size and strength are quite something to witness. Now you'll understand, Ms. Lilura.

"Do you see what she's doing?" Tommy yelled out until the last word was practically a snarl. There was panic setting in with the others as they spun around and tried to avoid the thin rhizomes from wrapping around their ankles. "Is this what you want? A witch to invade our territory and—"

Out of nowhere, a growl unlike any other I've ever heard from any of other werewolf came from the woods to the left of us. A massive lycanthrope suddenly made an appearance and somehow managed to plant itself no more than ten feet away from Matt.

This new visitor's frame was easily one and a half times that of the largest werewolf I'd ever seen in person. His chest was nearly four feet wide, and he was standing at least fourteen feet slightly crouched. Several weak territorial growls and snarls were made from the others, but at least no one had gone for the enormous animal standing before their Alpha.

This lycanthrope was clearly from the grey wolf species, much like the rest of the pack, yet his proportions were dramatically larger. His canines were as large as nine-inch nails and ten times as thick. He could easily palm the entire head of a normal werewolf. An attack against him would be completely reckless.

That was a grand entrance, was it not? Has the temperature gotten a bit warmer up on this mountain or what? Oh, my.

The colossal beast towered over the Alpha as if he were nothing but a mere mortal. The others had frozen in their tracks, giving the spell I'd been casting a chance to really grab hold. Those lycanthropes who'd been on the edge of our perimeter were now neutralized, allowing us the ability to deal with the problem child at hand— Tommy Sutter.

The gradual change from werewolf to man was not fully made, but Knox was now recognizable as he addressed the Alpha. The rumble of a vehicle was barely perceptible behind us as the snarls continued from those werewolves now trapped by the influence of magic. They were tearing at the strong hold of the vines and branches that were wrapped around their hairy ankles. With each vine they managed to break free, three more took its place.

That's a very unique way of diffusing a situation, dear hexed one. It's good to know that you can think outside the box.

"You don't belong here, Solitarius," Matt declared, the claws on his hand extending in his vain effort to regain control of the situation. I give him credit for not directly backing down to Knox's obvious advantage, but even I could see he was far out of his depth. He had no choice but to put on a show for his betas. "This is pack business, so take your human pets—"

"Enough," I called out, stepping away from Orwin when Knox growled to signify that he wasn't going to be intimidated by the Alpha's façade. Why would he? Pearl was right in that he was a sight to behold. "We came to this town to ensure that Noah Martin was safe. Bring him to us—unharmed—and we'll be on our way."

Pearl had finally shown herself and stayed glued to my side as I walked forward, not showing an ounce of fear. Knox could no doubt take six of these creatures with one massive paw tied behind his back. He could also just take the route of assuming control of the pack by simply destroying their Alpha. It helped to know we now had a healer on hand.

From the renewed round of growls behind me, she'd just joined the party.

My sweet Piper has, in fact, joined us. She's just so happened to discover what happened at the summer camp that ultimately resulted in what we are witnessing today.

"Tommy and his two friends discovered your secret when you were young, didn't they, Matt?" Piper called out as she finally came to stand beside Orwin. A quick glance reassured me that she held the ampule that would come in handy should things turn sour. "So, you did the only thing you could—you made a pledge to change them later in life in exchange for them keeping your secret."

I must say that Mr. Cornelia's program he wrote to search the internet for information was superb. No wonder scientists are saying that technology is going to weaken our ability to reason for ourselves. Critical thinking will become obsolete, if it hasn't already fulfilled their prophesy.

"Wait," Orwin directed with a frown. "What do you mean obsolete?"

Chapter Fifteen

"NOT THE TIME, guys," I murmured before closing the remaining distance to where Knox was still half wolf. It was inordinately creepy to see him in this manner, but it was better to have him on our side. "Matt, I realize that you followed through on your promise to keep your pack safe. I'm not here to cast judgement on anyone's motives. We only want Noah to come out of this unharmed."

Tommy growled, but Knox met his snarl with a deep-throated response of his own. The smaller werewolf immediately recoiled, managing to lose his footing in the bargain. It wasn't long before he was lying on the ground at our feet as a naked human.

Good heavens, cover that man. I could make a fortune teaching etiquette classes to these hairy beasts. Their parents would thank me endlessly.

Mason Leeds was the one to toss Tommy his clothes, but the distraction allowed me to finish our business here without bloodshed. I slowly raised my hands, allowing the rhizomes to release their hold on the remaining lycanthropes.

"I released your pack in good faith, Matt." I could sense Orwin and Piper taking up a position on either side of me until the five of us stood in a row of solidarity. "Let us take Noah with us, and we'll see that he's returned safely to his family. Haven't Lisa and the others suffered enough loss already?"

Well done, dear hexed one.

"They'll be told soon enough," Matt replied with resignation, giving Jasper a nod. None of us were expecting Chucky to walk out of the cabin with a big smile on his freckled face. "As I've said multiple times, I have things well in hand. The change is always difficult, and emotions run high. There's a reason I haven't allowed Tommy, Mason, and Clyde to leave the area. They'll only do so when I believe they're ready to be on their own. As for their immediate families, it will ultimately be their own choice to go with them if they so desire. Should they turn down that option, Chucky will ensure their memories are erased so that no harm comes to my pack in the end."

"Hi, Piper," Chucky called out with a wave, seemingly oblivious to the tension in the air.

Ah, Mr. Freckles is a warlock. Once again, this serves to teach us all that I should not remain behind on a scouting mission.

"Tommy escaped the confines of the cabin last night, and you were the one to track him down at the campsite," I ventured after having carefully thought through the last twenty-four hours. "He was going to kill Noah, but it was you who confronted me while he took off running back into the woods after seeing so many people."

It feels good to have a win in our pocket, does it not?

"Tommy doesn't trust witches or warlocks," Matt said wryly, still eyeing Knox with distrust. "He acted impulsively. I can't say I blame him, but this is my territory and my pack. There will be no innocent blood spilt here. Unfortunately, Chucky is still somewhat on a learning curve when it comes to your profession."

What Matt didn't know was that I'd seen the end of last night's confrontation. It *had* ended with blood spilt, and Noah was a very lucky man to be alive. Had we not been able to drive the eighteen hours in the RV, Lisa would have been burying her boyfriend alongside her brother.

I'm feeling now would be a good time for a knock-knock joke, dear hexed one. You're ignoring the silver lining, as usual. Mr. Martin is still alive, and we have the ability to wipe his memory clean so that he may return to his loved ones unscathed and of no danger to the pack.

"I'll do it," Piper said, casting a look toward Orwin that suggested he should go with her. "We'll also take Noah back to town and deliver him to safety on our way back to the campsite."

That is my sweet Piper's way of saying she doesn't trust Matt's control over these lycanthropes.

Matt practically roared when Tommy made a move to stop Piper, which immediately forced Knox to change as he sprang forward in protection. Mason and Clyde immediately retreated, while Tommy cowered on the ground under Knox's massive towering frame. A groan of pain escaped his lips as he grabbed his thigh. Now that his adrenaline was wearing off, the painful sting of his injury was breaking through.

"Tommy is still early in the transition," I pointed out, not necessarily willing to have Piper heal this blackmailing predator. Werewolves were able to heal themselves rather quickly, but Tommy's body was still adjusting to the transition. It could take a while before the wound closed shut. We could still offer some respite in exchange for what brought us here to begin with. "Piper can take care of that injury for Tommy, but do we have agreement on Noah Martin?"

It's very nice of you to feign that you've left Mr. Matt a choice, Ms. Lilura. He may keep his reputation intact among his pack, while we aid in getting this town back to some semblance of normal. Although, I must say...I don't like the way Mr. Chucky is grinning at my sweet Piper. Perhaps I shall turn him into a—

"You'll do no such thing," I reprimanded quietly, waiting for Matt to make his choice. Technically, there was only one decision to make in this complicated circumstance we'd found ourselves in, so I went ahead and cut the tension even more. "Piper, please assist Tommy with his injury. Orwin, would you please go inside the cabin with Chucky and rectify our small issue with Noah? Knox, um, do you have any…"

Mr. Knox, your clothes are folded in the back seat of your Land Rover. Thank you for being modest and remaining in wolf form. It's good to see that not all werewolves are disrespectful fiends devoid of a sense of modesty. Now, I'm off to have a conversation with Chucky about where his thoughts have strayed off to. Naughty boy, that one.

"Tommy, let this witch do her magic," Matt ordered, narrowing his now darkened eyes in warning. The werewolves on the edge of the perimeter had taken their Alpha's lead and returned completely to their human form. "Jasper, see to it that Miss…"

"Allifair," Piper chimed in with a bright smile, beginning to pull her gloves off. "Tommy, this won't hurt a bit, I promise."

"Thank you, Miss Allifair." One by one, everyone went their separate ways until I was standing alone with Matt. He'd made sure that everyone was following orders and giving us our space before addressing me. "Your friend is quite an exception. He is destined to be alone forever, thus the *nom de guerre*, Solitarius Lupus. He is most cursed amongst the children of the wolf, or so it is said in the legend. I trust you'll be leaving at sunset."

I would have to ask Orwin to look up this Solitarius Lupus. It was clear I needed to brush up my legends. One thing I could agree on was that Knox was quite something in his wolf form. Right now, it was time to clear up some things.

"You were ten years old when you made a deal with those three other youngsters. Why would you keep it when you knew what kind of exposure you were bringing to your pack?"

"A promise is a promise, and I wouldn't have the loyalty of my pack if I didn't follow through on my word…even a pact made years ago." Matt made it a point to look at Piper and then at the door of the cabin where Orwin had just disappeared in its shadow. I found it interesting that he didn't include Knox in the group, but I understood why given what we'd both witnessed. "You would do the same for those who follow you. We're a lot more alike than you realize, Ms. Lilura."

I wasn't so sure about his deduction, but he was a stranger, after all. I wasn't going to share my personal details or trials and tribulations with someone I would likely never see again. Trust had become quite elusive after my run in with Ammeline, but today proved that I had faith in those I surrounded myself with. The conclusion of this afternoon's confrontation gave me hope that Knox and I might very well succeed in finding a cure to our hexes—with a lot of help from our friends, of course.

"Jasper mentioned this happened five years ago."

"Unfortunately, one of ours went rogue," Matt answered regretfully, but at least he'd been truthful. "It happens from time to time, but we deal with them as a pack."

For a brief moment, I thought Matt was going to say family. This pack was his family, just as I'd come to have one of my own that now included a werewolf. We were an odd bunch, but we had each other's backs.

"We'll take Noah back to town and make sure that anything remotely leading him to the belief that your kind exists is wiped from his memory." I wasn't comfortable with Tommy and his friends' decision with how they handled their families, but some things were out of my control. "I'll have Orwin run through a few things with Chucky before we leave to make sure you don't have any trouble in the future ridding yourself of inconvenient memories."

"I appreciate that," Matt replied, his wary gaze landing on Knox as he emerged from the Land Rover completely dressed—including his brown leather bomber jacket. "You understand that he's not like us."

Matt wasn't talking about the species Knox had been created from, but rather that his change had been crafted through a powerful curse. Of course, he could only sense that Knox was different. This Alpha had no idea that a hex cast by a Lich was responsible, and I wanted to keep it that way.

"No," I agreed, closely observing Knox as he came closer. "He's not. Knox is more like me than he is like you."

Orwin and Pearl emerged from the cabin with Noah

in a stupor. Piper finished healing Tommy's injury just as Knox reached my side. It wasn't long before we were all side by side, Pearl looking especially pleased while Noah looked at everyone with the curiosity of a newborn babe. He wouldn't remember a thing a half an hour from now, but I sure hope that Pearl left Chucky in one piece to finish what was started here.

No worries, dear hexed one. Chucky and I have come to an understanding. I'm assuming the same was done with you and the Alpha. Shall we finally take our leave?

"Matt, we wish you well." I held out my hand in mutual respect, appreciating that he returned my gesture.

"And I, you. You'll need it."

It's so nice to witness a respectful exchange.

"You should take your own advice, Pearl," Orwin complained, walking toward the Jeep with Noah by his side. "Critical thinking is obsolete? I can't believe you would say something so horrendous."

Are you still stuck on that, alien hunter? I'm beginning to believe Ms. Lilura is rubbing off on you. Neither one of you can take a joke to save your lives, and that is very important in this complicated journey we're all on.

"Pearl, I'm pretty sure it was your timing," Piper chimed in, playing peacemaker once more.

"Do I want to know what they're saying?" Knox asked guardedly, falling beside me as we closed the distance to the vehicles. "Never mind. I'm better off not knowing."

I glanced over my shoulder to see Tommy standing

with his two friends, looking quite contrite in front of Matt now that the heated confrontation had been diffused. Sheriff Jacobs was staring at his vehicle in horror, and Jasper remained on the porch watching us a bit too closely. I'm sure the older lycanthrope wanted us out of the area pronto. We would oblige him, because we had places to be and people to see…about a hex.

"Knox, how would you feel about joining us on a road trip to Minnesota?" I asked, comfortable now with the extended offer. After all, we had a common goal in mind and working together would produce more results. "There's a medium who could help contact the other side in search of answers to our…shared problem."

Knox waited until we came to the Jeep, where Orwin was guiding Noah into the back seat. Piper was now holding Pearl, and we all regarded Knox closely as he finally gave us his decision.

"A road trip to Minnesota to see a medium?" Knox asked with a small smile. He rubbed the five o'clock shadow covering his jawline, as if he had a stipulation. I hadn't expected him to ask for something in return, so I tensed while waiting to hear his demand. Maybe this wasn't going to work out, after all. "I've had a crash course in the supernatural. I'm well aware that witches, warlocks, and vampires exist, along with the naturally occurring version of my own kind. Mediums and dead ancestors? I've got to tell you, I'm not a big fan of ghosts and ghouls."

"Oh, ghosts and ghouls definitely exist," I confirmed with a smile. It was nice to see that Knox was trying to take his curse in stride. A ray of hope in this overcast day found its way through to my soul. If we all stuck together, there was a really good chance we could come out intact on the other side of this whole thing. "Don't worry, though. We'll protect you."

Knox's rich laughter filled the air. Piper fished his keys out of her jacket and tossed them to him, mindful of Pearl in her other arm. It was a safe bet she had yet tell him of the damage she'd done to his wiring. After promising to meet us back at the campsite, he took his leave.

"I like him," Piper quipped, calling shotgun so that she didn't have to sit in the backseat with Noah. She opened the door and climbed inside, setting Pearl on her lap. "Another team member. And he's a rather large werewolf. Go figure."

I'm in agreement, my sweet Piper. He knows how to laugh, despite his fate.

I tried not to roll my eyes at Pearl's dig, but I utterly failed. I was grateful when Orwin chimed in, saving me from having to answer her. It wasn't as if I didn't know how to laugh, but there had to be a reason, right?

"Emeric seems nice and all," Orwin said in regard to the new arrangements, "but I'm really glad he's driving in his own vehicle. Pearl's dander is about as much as I can take inside the RV. Oh, by the way, I ordered an air purifying system for the RV. It will be waiting for us when we arrive at the next major town on the way to Minnesota. I rented a mailbox there, and I already mapped out our route."

Let me guess. You have us traveling through Wisconsin, alien hunter. Belleville, to be precise.

"Maybe." Orwin pushed up his glasses with a frown, but we all accepted that the campsite would be near a UFO sighting. I'd forgotten to warn Knox about Orwin's conspiracy theorist tendencies, but he'd find out soon enough. Then again, Knox had been following us for the past four months. He'd probably already figured it out. "Okay. We're definitely stopping in Belleville. Let's hit the road. This is going to be great!"

Not so fast, Pearl hedged. *Knock-knock.*

"Pearl, is now really the time to—"

Knock-knock, dear hexed one.

"Answer her, Lou," Piper said with a smile. "It's the only way we're getting out of here, and this one is way better than the witch walked into a bar joke. Trust me."

"Fine," I sighed in resignation, resting my hands on my hips while I waited for the punchline. "Who's there?"

Witch.

Of course, it was a witch. Piper gave me a nod of encouragement to keep going, so I did.

"Witch, who?"

Witch one of you will be driving us out of this doggone town?

~ THE END ~

Thank you so much for continuing to follow the *Hex on Me Mysteries* with Lou and the gang! The next thrilling tale—*The Squeaky Ghost Gets the Curse*—involves a haunted house and a rather loud ghost…and this is one story that you won't want to miss!

kennedylayne.com/the-squeaky-ghost-gets-the-curse.html

Things go bump in the night in this hauntingly riveting tale in the Hex on Me Mysteries by USA Today Bestselling Author Kennedy Layne…

Lou can't even manage to dip a chocolate chip cookie into her glass of cold milk without getting a premonition of murder. Her unsettling vision is different this time around, though. The victim was practically thrown down a spiral staircase by…an invisible force right out of thin air!

Lou has no doubt that a murder was committed, and now it's a race against time to determine why. Unfortunately, Lou and the gang know they'll be too late to stop an affluent widow from meeting her fate. All they can do is figure out who killed the reclusive woman in order to give her grown children some sort of closure while saving them from a similar fate.

All is not what it seems, though. As things begin to go bump in the night and strange noises eerily echo throughout the ancient mansion, Lou is left wondering if the culprit isn't a vengeful spirit with a purpose. You might want to keep the lights on for this scary ghost story—it promises to be a jumping cool time!

BOOKS BY KENNEDY LAYNE

HEX ON ME MYSTERIES
If the Curse Fits
Cursing up the Wrong Tree
The Squeaky Ghost Gets the Curse

PARAMOUR BAY MYSTERIES
Magical Blend
Bewitching Blend
Enchanting Blend
Haunting Blend
Charming Blend
Spellbinding Blend
Cryptic Blend

OFFICE ROULETTE SERIES
Means (Office Roulette, Book One)
Motive (Office Roulette, Book Two)
Opportunity (Office Roulette, Book Three)

KEYS TO LOVE SERIES
Unlocking Fear (Keys to Love, Book One)
Unlocking Secrets (Keys to Love, Book Two)
Unlocking Lies (Keys to Love, Book Three)
Unlocking Shadows (Keys to Love, Book Four)
Unlocking Darkness (Keys to Love, Book Five)

SURVIVING ASHES SERIES
Essential Beginnings (Surviving Ashes, Book One)
Hidden Ashes (Surviving Ashes, Book Two)

Buried Flames (Surviving Ashes, Book Three)
Endless Flames (Surviving Ashes, Book Four)
Rising Flames (Surviving Ashes, Book Five)

CSA CASE FILES SERIES
Captured Innocence (CSA Case Files 1)
Sinful Resurrection (CSA Case Files 2)
Renewed Faith (CSA Case Files 3)
Campaign of Desire (CSA Case Files 4)
Internal Temptation (CSA Case Files 5)
Radiant Surrender (CSA Case Files 6)
Redeem My Heart (CSA Case Files 7)
A Mission of Love (CSA Case Files 8)

RED STARR SERIES
Starr's Awakening(Red Starr, Book One)
Hearths of Fire (Red Starr, Book Two)
Targets Entangled (Red Starr, Book Three)
Igniting Passion (Red Starr, Book Four)
Untold Devotion (Red Starr, Book Five)
Fulfilling Promises (Red Starr, Book Six)
Fated Identity (Red Starr, Book Seven)
Red's Salvation (Red Starr, Book Eight)

THE SAFEGUARD SERIES
Brutal Obsession (The Safeguard Series, Book One)
Faithful Addiction (The Safeguard Series, Book Two)
Distant Illusions (The Safeguard Series, Book Three)
Casual Impressions (The Safeguard Series, Book Four)
Honest Intentions (The Safeguard Series, Book Five)
Deadly Premonitions (The Safeguard Series, Book Six)

ABOUT THE AUTHOR

First and foremost, I love life. I love that I'm a wife, mother, daughter, sister… and a writer.

I am one of the lucky women in this world who gets to do what makes them happy. As long as I have a cup of coffee (maybe two or three) and my laptop, the stories evolve themselves and I try to do them justice. I draw my inspiration from a retired Marine Master Sergeant that swept me off of my feet and has drawn me into a world that fulfills all of my deepest and darkest desires. Erotic romance, military men, intrigue, with a little bit of kinky chili pepper (his recipe), fill my head and there is nothing more satisfying than making the hero and heroine fulfill their destinies.

Thank you for having joined me on their journeys…

Email: kennedylayneauthor@gmail.com

Facebook: facebook.com/kennedy.layne.94

Twitter: twitter.com/KennedyL_Author

Website: www.kennedylayne.com

Newsletter:
www.kennedylayne.com/aboutnewsletter.html